Death Has Seven Faces

Death Has Seven Faces

Hugh Austin

COACHWHIP PUBLICATIONS
Greenville, Ohio

Death has Seven Faces, by Hugh Austin
© 2022 Coachwhip Publications edition

First published 1949
Hugh Austin Evans, 1903-1964
CoachwhipBooks.com

ISBN 1-61646-523-9
ISBN-13 978-1-61646-523-0

1

The old Chinaman stood with bent knees, his thin shoulders hunched under his white jacket, his wizened head cocked to one side with one eye tight shut and the other screwed to the eyepiece of the long brass telescope that was mounted on the window sill. From five thousand feet below the window, and thirty miles away, the telescope brought to its eyepiece the glare of the shimmering desert. The old man drew back his head and rubbed at a watery eye. Behind him in the room there was a whispered warning from the man in the bed.

"It's time, Sin. It's time."

The old Chinaman again screwed his eye to the telescope. Again the only sound in the room was the labored breathing of the dying man. From five thousand feet below the window, and thirty miles away, into the bright circle of the telescope there crawled a thin dark worm. The old man again drew back his head. He turned his walnut-shell face from the window.

"Tlain come."

From her Pullman window Helen Farr watched the mountain range roll towards her over the desert. On the south shore of Long Island she had upon a few stormy occasions seen great waves roll over the sandy beach from which there would have been no wading out again had she gone within reach of them. In her lap her fingers tightened upon the letter that had brought her from that Atlantic shore to this Arizona desert. . . . *I am alone and dying, Helen, alone . . .*

The glint of sunlight on the brass telescope caught Captain McIntyre's eye as he turned in his pacing at the corner of the lodge. He jerked his shoulders and kicked at a stone. Laced boots and riding breeches with a khaki shirt and black necktie contributed to something nostalgically military in his appearance; a checked jacket, something racy. He was a man nearing fifty with thin brown hair and a toothbrush mustache. His long narrow face ended in a square and outthrust chin. His jaw was clenched when he turned in his pacing at the corner of the lodge.

His upward glance and his following kick at the stone had been noticed by Sylvia Cole as she reclined in seemingly indolent ease in a chair with a footrest in front of the lodge. Her almond eyes turned from him to the man seated beside her, weighing their strength.

Not physically, there was no question of that. Though George Sears was by ten years the elder man, with only a glint of red remaining in his gray hair, he was six-feet-three in height and of an unusually powerful build. As he sat at ease in his chair with his square hands lying on his heavy thighs he had the solid calm of a stone statue. Even the texture of his gray-brown skin, pitted by smallpox, was like that of unpolished granite. Sylvia Cole found it as inscrutable.

Her eyes returned to Harry McIntyre's drawn face as he returned on the terrace, seeing that in the tension of these last hours of waiting, after a week of waiting, it might not take much more to strain to the breaking point the guard which he had been keeping upon his thoughts. She smiled at him as if amused.

"Now sit down and stop fretting," she said soothingly, as to a child. And as to a child she added, "Father isn't worried."

Harry McIntyre stopped short in front of her.

"Has Jay forgotten that Saul was in love with her mother?" he demanded. His clipped voice was exasperated. "I tell you the rest of us are likely to find ourselves holding the bag."

Red Sears slowly turned his head. He said quietly, "I think Saul knows us well enough not to try to leave her more than a fair share."

Sylvia Cole became aware that he was looking at her and she realized that his words had not been an indiscretion but had been spoken so that he might try to judge how far she could be trusted. She shrugged her shoulders. Her turquoise sweater was becoming both to her figure and her dark beauty.

"The daughter isn't the mother," she pointed out to Harry McIntyre. "And he hasn't even seen her since she was a child. There's simply no reason for him to leave her more than a sentimental remembrance."

She was relieved to see that George Sears was again gazing out over the abandoned mine.

. . . *All is now desolation at Dead Finger Fault. Only Sin remains unchanged. It is strangely fitting that that faithful servant of your father's who came to me after Frederick's death should now attend my deathbed. Because now, an old man alone and dying, I must confess to you that I planned and profited by the venture that bankrupted your father and drove him to suicide. May God forgive me. My only excuse is that I had been in love with your mother before Frederick married her and was mad with jealousy. Now I cannot die in peace until I make restitution to you of all that is rightfully yours. . . .* She had known every word of the infirm handwriting by heart for days, but, as ever, Helen Farr searched for something between the lines which she felt escaped her.

She looked up at the Pullman porter.

"Sasoon in five minutes, Miss."

As Jay Warren Cole turned from the railroad station to cross the hundred yards of sunbaked earth between him and the main street of the town his eyes swept quickly up and down the three short blocks of frame and adobe buildings petering out into the desert at either end. A half dozen automobiles were strung along the roadway and a dozen and a half people under the porch roofs that shaded the board sidewalk. His furtive glance recognized one or two who stood talking with friends, and then careful to glance neither to the right nor to the left he marched forward with a beaming face.

It was a red full moon of a face with small pouched eyes and a parrot's nose, with triple chins spreading wide the points of the turned-up collar of his gray flannel shirt and lapping over the knot of the necktie encircling the turned-up collar with a band of gold and black stripes, while encircling the barrel waist of the twill riding breeches that he was wearing with knee-high hobnailed boots was a belt covered with the skin of a diamondback rattlesnake. Not inconspicuous, indomitably smiling, he went in a straight line to the bar room of the Sasoon Hotel.

He found Nicholas Baron and Jeffery Oliphant still standing where he had left them at the front end of the bar with a clear view of the yellow and brown railroad station. The two cousins bore no family resemblance. Nick Baron was a black-haired and bold-featured man in his first thirties. He was wearing a sports shirt, slacks and golf shoes. Before driving to town that day from the mine, the mine to which in years past Jay Warren Cole had contributed so many hopeful investors, his comment upon their respective costumes had been, "All I need's a putter; and you, a sucker." His smile, the lower lip curling out, was now equally frank in its gibing amusement.

Jeff Oliphant continued to gaze out the windows towards the station. Perhaps a year or two younger than his cousin Nick, as tall but of a heavier build, his blunt-featured face left no question of his distaste for his company. He took off his battered brown hat and replaced it at an angle that shut out the sight of them.

Blandly beaming, Jay Warren Cole dropped his own wide-brimmed and high-crowned hat on the bar and patted a handkerchief around his fringe of gray hair while waiting for a glass of beer. He drank deeply, smacked his lips and sighed.

"Nectar, my dear young friends!" he declaimed. "Nectar."

He jiggled his glass in time to a tune from the radio until the bartender went to the far end of the bar and resumed an earnest conversation with the only other customer. Then, very casually, he explained his return from the station platform.

"A parching sun, gentlemen," he said. "Parching!" He smiled at his cool glass. "I decided not to wait."

Nick Baron nodded. "Price does have big feet." Cole chuckled so heartily that his shoulders shook and the beer sloshed in his glass.

"Well, indeed, I could almost feel one of them landing on my posterior!" he admitted handsomely, and put an end to the embarrassing fact.

"Not that we're critical," Nick said. "We'd try to butt in too if we thought Price would start reading the will to her when she gets off the train."

Jay Warren Cole hoped that he sensed a guarded invitation for a meeting of minds. It would be a delicate negotiation through pitfalls of mutual suspicion yet a thing requiring a certain boldness in execution.

"But surely you've no reason to be doubtful of Saul's intentions?" he asked, feeling his way. "His own nephews!"

he protested. "Surely you can't think that he'd favor the daughter of those who were mere friends over"—his florid tones gave the words a rococo richness—"his own flesh and blood?"

He smiled and shrugged and sighed that such things had been known to be.

"Frankly," he said, and he was a blunt man, a bluff old fellow who came straight out with plain words, "frankly," he said, "we're in the same boat," and by the manner in which he looked at the floor it was clear that it was leaking. He opened his hands on the bar as if spreading his cards on the table. "You have the just claims of family," he conceded. He added, as a matter of course, "I have a just claim. Now of course we're deeply grateful to Saul! Deeply grateful. But," he admitted, "we do have some right to be here." He went a step farther. "I think I might even say that we have claims that must come before sentiment." He paused to measure his last words carefully that their insinuation might be clear and yet remain only an insinuation. "Such claims are not to be set aside by anyone. It might be unfortunate," he concluded, "if Saul should forget that."

Jeff Oliphant said, "He can forget anything if he can forget fourteen years in prison."

Nick Baron grinned as he saw Cole stop smiling in a way that gave a sickly look to his florid face. None of them spoke again while they waited.

On the station platform Willet Price was standing alone when the train came to a stop in a swirl of hot wind and alkali dust. The gust of air fluttered the straight brim of his gray felt hat, plucked at the lapels of his gray business suit, and then subsiding left a powdering of gray dust on his dull black shoes. He stood with his bony hands lightly clasped behind his back while he unhurriedly sized up the only passenger to get off the train.

He saw that she could easily be taken to be even somewhat younger than her age which he knew to be twenty-six. She was moderately tall and her figure was on the slender side. He noticed with indifference that she was wearing a trimly tailored green suit and that there was a glimpse of coppery hair under a jaunty knockabout hat. Details of her appearance were in his opinion unimportant, but that they resulted in her being a very attractive young woman might not be, not while there were men in the world or at the mine. Her personality was a matter of his more immediate concern and he noted that her mouth gave an impression of warmth and sensitivity. He also noted that she had an erect carriage and that the profile of her face was clear and crisp. He decided that she was a pleasant person but one with a certain amount of spirit. Well, he would soon find how much and of what kind. When her eyes met his he walked slowly forward removing his hat from his pewter-gray hair.

"Miss Farr? I'm Willet Price."

"Thank you for meeting me!" There was, as he had anticipated, an engaging friendliness in her voice. The look in her eyes, they were a darker gray than his own, was also unguarded. "I've addressed so many letters in your care," she continued, "that it seems I should have known you since childhood!" Her face sobered. "How is Mr. Baron?" she asked.

Willet Price said, "He was still alive when the car left the mine." He gave her time to swallow it, like a dry pill. "As soon as the mail's picked up," he resumed, "you'll be driven out. Would you like to wait in my office?"

"Why, yes. Thank you." She felt something that was at least not friendly in his dry courtesy. It was blankly disconcerting in that first moment of her arrival. He put on his hat and picked up her suitcase and dressing case.

"Have you a trunk?" he asked. A steamer trunk, she told him. "Then we may as well leave these here until you pick up the trunk in the car." He set the bags on a bench against the side of the station and turned towards the town.

As they walked away Helen Farr glanced once over her shoulder to see her bags sitting abandoned on the bench and the Pullmans of the limited moving out of the station. Ahead of her was the strangeness of the tiny town on a wide plain under an immense and empty sky. She felt very far from home and very much alone.

The shingle of *Willet Price, Attorney at Law* hung above a doorway on the corner opposite the Sasoon Hotel. At the top of a straight flight of worn wooden stairs was a bleak room covered by a film of gritty dust. It was on the bare wood floor and it was on the golden oak sectional bookcases filled with specimens of ore, legal tomes and book-shaped correspondence files, and, annoyingly, it was on the seat and arms of the chair that the lawyer offered her.

She sat on the edge of the chair, her back straight, her well-shod feet close together, as if on the point of rising again. Her manner had become a shade more stand-offish than his own. He sat down facing her, his left arm lying on the open front of his rolltop desk, his bony fingers hooked over a crystal of quartz that served as a paperweight.

"Saul was afraid that you might not come," he said.

"He need not have been."

"You are very forgiving."

"Thank you."

Willet Price turned the quartz paperweight in his long fingers. "I did not mean that as a criticism," he said.

Oh, yes, you did, Helen thought. But with his apology her temper went down. She was not surprised that Saul Baron, on the point of death, had confided to his old attorney his reason for making her his beneficiary. On her part she had no reluctance to explain how she felt about that confession.

"From the time I can remember anything," she said, "my 'Uncle' Saul had always been kindness itself to me. And after my mother's death . . . It may seem strange when I have not seen him since then, but in some ways he became the closest person in the world to me. His letters—you know how many—were so wonderfully understanding that I came to feel that I could write to him little secrets that I couldn't even tell my aunt with whom I lived. Then to learn that when I was four years old . . . that it was because of him that I have no memory of my father . . ."

Helen Farr shook her head. "I hate to see him," she admitted. "I hated to come. But when I think of him as he is now . . ." *alone and dying . . . alone . . .* "Of course I wouldn't have come otherwise." Her voice became bitter. "And to think that it was such a disappointment to me all these years that he'd always find some excuse for not coming to New York to see me or, since I've grown up, to let me visit him."

Willet Price said, "That was quite impossible."

"Yes, of course. I realize now that it was because he couldn't face me."

The lawyer continued to look at the quartz crystal. He gave it a slight turn in his fingers.

"Physically impossible," he said.

"I don't understand."

Willet Price again turned the crystal, studied another facet.

"You've always written him in care of me," he said.

"Yes. He was always traveling so much."

"Saul always wrote to you in longhand?"

"Why—yes, I think so."

He raised his head. She followed his gaze to the dusty cover of a typewriter.

"But the addresses of the envelopes mailed to you were always typewritten," he reminded her. "By me," he added.

"By you! Why?"

Willet Price looked at her with eyes as expressionless as the quartz crystal.

"Because for fourteen years," he said dryly, "Saul has been writing to you from prison."

For a moment all that it meant to Helen Farr was that it swept every thought from her mind. For the first time since she had entered the office she became aware of sounds below the open windows . . . an indistinct snatch of voices . . . the slam of a car door . . . some one whistling. . . .

"—Sentences did not run concurrently."

He had, Helen knew, although she had not consciously listened to him, said something before that because it was now in her knowledge that Saul Baron had been convicted of fraud in the sale of stock in the mine and of embezzlement of funds in its operation, convicted and sent to prison. Her thoughts returned to that word, its meaning. Then another of the lawyer's dry phrases caught at her attention.

"Obviously as a convict he couldn't continue a correspondence with a child, aside from the fact that your aunt would never have permitted it. That was the reason for the deception."

Her thoughts had been on a man in a prison cell. The man was writing a letter to a child; he was describing the funniest and most exciting thing that had just happened to him the other day when he had been out riding. The man was writing a letter to an adolescent schoolgirl; he was relating the most remarkable story about the most romantic young man that he had just met the other day on a trip to Old Mexico. The man was writing a letter to a young woman; he was being wonderfully understanding and sympathetic about the little problem which she had

confided to him in her last letter, and he was deeply re-
gretful that he could not visit her this summer but he had
to make a prolonged trip into the mountains to look at a
new mining property. . . Her thoughts had been on that
man in the cell who year after year for fourteen years had
projected himself out of that cell to capture the love of a
child and hold it through the years, and she had felt her
heart contract for him.

"That was the reason for the deception."

Deception. That was the other side of the coin, and it
brought Helen Farr up short.

"Saul would have told you all this in his last letter," the
lawyer's voice continued, "except that he was afraid that it
might tip the scales against your coming here."

Deception. More deception. "It might," she said in a
tone as dry as Willet Price's own, "have made me wonder
if Mr. Baron was really so greatly changed from the man
who deceived my father."

Willet Price ignored it. "Saul's been very anxiously
awaiting you," he said. "You're the last one to arrive."

"The last one?"

"Yes."

"I still don't understand what you mean, Mr. Price." . . .
I am alone and dying, alone . . . "Isn't Mr. Baron alone?"

"No," Willet Price said with a faint smile. "Saul's told
me that he neglected to mention it in his letter to you,
but his nephews, Mr. Jeffery Oliphant and Mr. Nicholas
Baron, are here."

"His nephews?" Helen repeated. "I've never known before that he had any living relatives at all." The lawyer's
smile was slight but she felt that he was laughing at her.

"I can see where the appearance of two unsuspected
'cousins' is a surprise," he said. "But, in fact, they're in
town with Mr. Cole to take you back with them to the
mine."

She said evenly, "I'm afraid that he also forgot to mention that Mr. Cole was here."

"Why, yes," Willet Price affirmed. "Mr. Cole and his daughter have been waiting at Dead Finger for over a week. It will be pleasant for you to have another young woman about your own age for company," he added considerately.

"Very pleasant."

"Saul must have mentioned Mr. Cole to you years ago in his letters?" Price suggested. "Or when he used to visit you and your mother in New York? Possibly you remember?"

Memory brought a smile, a relaxation of her tension.

"'Old King Cole was a merry old soul,'" she said. "A child is not likely to forget a name like that. And then there was a 'Red George' who I always understood to be a giant like the one in 'Jack and the Beanstalk'?"

The lawyer inclined his gray head. "Mr. Sears was the mine superintendent."

"And when I was in my teens he used to write me fascinating things about a dashing Captain Harry—?"

"Captain McIntyre was the mining engineer. It was just a week ago that he arrived," Willet Price continued smoothly, "and Mr. Sears two days later."

Helen Farr opened her handbag and found a cigarette. He held a match for her.

"Thank you."

She could not stall any longer. "How many more people are there with Mr. Baron?" she asked.

Willet Price shook his head. "Aside from Sin and a boy who is helping him, there are just the seven of you."

"These former associates of his," she asked, facing it, "are they also former convicts?"

"No," Willet Price said, looking at her oddly. "No, they turned state's evidence at his trial."

Helen looked at him blankly for an awkward length of time.

"I'm sorry," she apologized, "but there's been so much that I've become confused. When you first spoke of them I thought you meant that they were here to receive—a legacy, I think it's called?"

"Why, yes, Miss Farr. Just as he sent for you."

She realized that her hand was trembling and wished that there was some place where she could get rid of the cigarette. Price, unhooking a long finger from the quartz crystal, pointed to the floor. He waited until she had rubbed it out underfoot and was again facing him before he continued with his explanation. "I thought you understood," he said, "that Saul is now a forgiving and a repentant man?"

"Yes," she said in a small voice, "he must be."

"A great spiritual change," Willet Price affirmed dryly. "You must try to understand that the old Saul Baron who never repaid a kindness or forgave an injury is now a repentant and a forgiving man."

It was then that Helen Farr became afraid. She said, obediently, "Yes, Mr. Price."

There was a slight thawing in the lawyer's manner. "I'm sorry that Saul didn't write you more fully," he said. "I don't know how much of the ground he did cover. He told you of his intended bequest, of course?"

"Yes, Mr. Price."

"And explained that it was necessary for you to be here in person to receive it?"

"Yes, Mr. Price. He said that unusual circumstances made my presence necessary. He did not explain what they were." It was not until she gave the answer that she realized that he had been trying to pump her.

"No doubt," he said, dismissing the subject, since she did not know the answer to it, "it's one of the many things that Saul has reserved to explain to you himself." He rose at the thrice-repeated sound of an automobile horn below the window. "I think you'll find your ride to Dead Finger very interesting," he said.

She rode beside Nick Baron on the front seat of an old touring car with her trunk on a rack behind and her bags in the back seat with Jeff Oliphant and Jay Warren Cole. Ten miles out of Sasoon the car turned off from the valley and within a mile the first foothill closed behind them like a softly closing door. With strangers in a strange country there was a disquieting sense of having been cut off with them from the rest of the world.

Jay Warren Cole had welcomed her with a beaming smile to their sorrowful, as he had termed it, company. As picturesque as Price was colorless, as effusively friendly as Price had been dryly hostile. Helen found him a somewhat overwhelming but a welcome change. He became her guide on the ride, naming flora and fauna, and pointing out the twin peaks of Dos Santos rising from the ragged crest of the range. He indicated the approximate position at the feet of the Two Saints where, appropriately enough, a repentant and forgiving man awaited their arrival.

Once within the threshold of the mountain the road weaved between desolate foothills and crossed arid flats where bushy-headed chollas brandished the long stalks of their spears as they stood on guard over their forbidding wasteland of mesquite and cactus. The flats became less than a mile wide, the foothills, spiked with Spanish bayonet, rose higher and more steeply. Helen saw prickly pears that looked like juggling acts with green pancakes; more cottontails started up in alarm only to freeze, peeking over their shoulders, and fewer jack rabbits loped away into the far distance of sun and solitude. At a great height in the brilliantly clear sky, seemingly as high as the lofty heads of the Two Saints, black specks wheeled and circled.

"Buzzards," Cole informed her, leaning forward to shout in her ear and then sinking back again.

"They always rally around when they smell death," Nick Baron took up the natural history lesson.

Whenever he glanced at her, which was as often as the road permitted, Helen was made aware that he wanted her to know that as a woman she attracted him. It was the boldly intimate look of one of those men who are confident that they are attractive to women. It annoyed her that she did find him attractive. It was also a warning to be careful. His smile, the lower lip curling out, had the same bold quality as his dark eyes, but it was strictly an amused smile, neither kindly nor friendly.

"First you'll see one buzzard up there waiting," he continued, "then another, then a whole flock from near"—he smiled at her—"and far."

Helen Farr took the slap in silence. Glancing over her left shoulder, her eyes met the cool blue gaze of Jeff Oliphant. She did not know what to make of his attitude towards her. She saw now that he was displeased by what Nick Baron had said, but that was no assurance that he did not also look upon her as a buzzard coming in at the death. She felt that he would, automatically, be displeased by anything that either Nick or Cole might say. That was her first warning of what lay ahead, the undercurrent of hostility that she sensed between the three men.

After the incident Jay Warren Cole abandoned his effort to cast a rosy social glow over the party with his florid friendliness, and they rode in a guarded silence broken only at long intervals by some impersonal comment, just to show that they were civilized. Within an hour they were winding between a succession of ever higher hills of tumbled granite, each more heavily wooded with green oaks, and then the road was climbing a spur of the

mountain proper and within another hour the road was a
ledge cut in the side of the mountain. It seemed to Helen
Farr like a road on the side of the roof of the world. Behind her the sun was no higher in the sky than she was and
the mountain top was radiant in sunlight that was clear
amber while a purple shadow lay over all the world below.

As she again turned her eyes to the road ahead the
thing happened. A hundred feet ahead, and about the same
distance above, the road part of the mountain side exploded into the air. The car lurched to a stop as blurs of rock
tore through the trees. Twenty feet ahead a boulder struck
the road and burst into white fragments. Another whirling
block struck the edge of the embankment on the uphill
side of the road and bounced over the car. The car vibrated
under some blow. There was a thudding hail of smaller
fragments of stone. Then there was silence broken only by
the rattle of loose slides of stone. A thin white cloud of
quartz dust and the biting smell of nitro fumes hung over
the road.

Helen had both arms raised in front of her face. The
jolting stop of the car had thrown her against Nick Baron's shoulder. When she sat up again she saw that he was
peering up the side of the mountain through the wind-
shield. Turning farther around, she saw Jeff's white, set
face raised towards a ragged hole in the fabric top of the
touring car.

"What's happened?" she asked in a dull whisper. "What
was that?"

Nick Baron sat back from the steering wheel.

"That . . ." he said, his eyes resting for a moment on a
sledge-hammer dent in the hood, "why, that would be Mr.
Parsons."

Helen teetered on the edge of hysterical laughter.

A firm hand was laid on her shoulder.

"Are you all right?" Jeff Oliphant asked. "You weren't hit?"

"No," she said. "No, I don't think so." Then, in quick anxiety, "Are you? Is any one?" She looked around her.

"What about it, Jay?" Jeff asked.

Helen saw Jay Warren Cole shake his head while his finger-tips dabbed at a slight cut on his cheekbone. Jeff took his hand from her shoulder but continued to look at her as if doubtful of her nerves.

"Mr. Parsons," he told her, "is an old prospector who's starting a drift in a vein of quartz he's staked up there."

"Mr. Parsons doesn't use a battery when he blasts," Nick said. He kept half an eye on Cole as if speaking as much for his benefit as her own. "He's lit the fuse and then gone on his way to his cabin to cook supper," he explained. "The fuse simply happened to burn down as we got here. Accidents like this are likely to happen in a mining country," he concluded, and having firmly ironed out any other possibilities he threw the car into gear. "I'm afraid I scraped a fender when I drew over to the curb," he said with a smile.

Helen looked over the side.

"I've done worse when parking for the movies," she assured him. Then she lost her temper. "And now that we've all been simply noble little ladies and gentlemen," she said icily, "I'd like to know if Mr. Parsons was waiting for us?"

The question caught Nick Baron by surprise and he did not like it.

"Why would he?" he asked shortly.

"Perhaps," Helen snapped, "he was just trying to kill two buzzards with one stone." She saw that only Jeff Oliphant smiled, and somewhat thinly.

A few minutes later Dead Finger Fault was ahead of her. The abandoned mine extended up both slopes at the head of a great gulch. The dumps of its tunnels and shafts made broad terraces with rusted ore cars forever waiting on rusted tracks. Above the trees stood conveyor towers

whose connecting cables had once carried ore skips overhead to the metal-sheathed stamp mill. The scale of the
operations that had been carried on, the vast wreckage of
hope that she saw before her, was her first glimpse of Saul
Baron.

The car, climbing steeply from the stampmill, came
to a stop on a terrace in front of a long, two-story lodge
finished in split logs. A girl and two men came forward.
. . . But Helen found her eyes held by the grinning face of
an old Chinaman. He continued to grin at her from what
had the look of a highly irascible face while he fished her
bags from the back seat, his grin blurring the impression
of those to whom she was introduced.

Sylvia Cole, dark and beautiful, a richly soft voice and
a warm friendliness of manner. . . . Mr. Sears, a giant with
a granite face, his voice as quiet as a whisper. . . . Captain
McIntyre, rather dissolute-looking, a clipped voice and a
clipped manner. . . .

There was the old stillness that came over all three of
them when they were told the cause of the damage to the
car and the abrasion on Cole's cheek. There was the way
Sylvia Cole turned not to her father but to Nick Baron.
Then there was the grinning face of the old Chinaman as
he summoned her to follow him by a jerk of his head.

He led her up an outside stairway at the near end of
the lodge. Helen glanced back only once. She saw a young
Chinese-American whose pleasant face had the "what the
hell, let's have some fun out of it" look of a college boy
on a vacation job. He was juggling a box of groceries from
the car while her six fellow guests stood in a silent group
waiting for both him and her to get out of hearing. At the
top of the stairs she had a brief look at a seventy-five-foot
hall swept by a cool breeze from another door, open to
another outside stairs at the far end, before she followed

her guide into the first bedroom to the right. He set down her luggage and stood grinning at her.

"I've always known you'd be exactly like this," Helen told him. "So don't try to tell me that you aren't Sin."

"Shule!" he assured her in a sing-song cackle of delight. "Shule, me Sin! How many moah old Flisco Chinaboy change youa dliapa when you baby, huh?" He was holding his hands as if holding a baby. He dropped the baby. "Now all glown up big and not so plink." He beamed at her from every wrinkle of his wizened face.

Helen wagged her head. "If I hadn't been told that, in fact, you refused to touch me with a ten-foot pole—!" She put her hand on his arm. "You're the nicest old family tradition I've ever met."

His Adam's apple went up and down. "You not too bad."

"To think you've been here alone all these years!"

"Oh, yes," he told her. "Stay heah all time keep house all leddy he come back." He cocked his head on one side, grinned wryly. "Now maybe betta we go," he admitted. "He no can wait too much longa."

He led the way across the hall and opened the door of the bedroom directly opposite her own. Like her own, the room was finished in pine mill work and was furnished in the square-legged, oak-stained style known as Mission. There was a bureau with a square mirror, an armchair with a leather cushion, and a small table at the head of the bed. On the table were a spoon in a tumbler, a gray medicine box and a watch lying face up.

In the bed a man was lying propped up by pillows. His head was large and bald. His face was white with sagging cheeks. His temples were sunken, brushed with shadow, and the skin was drawn tight over his nose so that it stood out like a sharp, predatory beak. But though it took no more than one glance at the face on the pillow to see that

Saul Baron was dead, the thin smile on his blue lips made
its dominant impression one of malignant vitality.

Helen had stopped short after closing the door while
Sin had slowly shuffled forward into the bedroom. She
forced herself to go to the side of the old man standing
with hunched shoulders at the foot of the bed. Her hand
touched his arm.

He turned his head slowly, his eyes for a moment still
seeing the face of the dead man, and then as he looked at
her the blank expression of his face and his eyes changed
startlingly in a flash of excitement that could have been
either of rage or of fear.

"Get hell outa heah!" he whispered fiercely. His mum-
my's hands pushed her backward towards the door. "Get
hell outa heah God damn light now!"

Helen put her hands on his shoulders, trying to calm
him.

"Please, Sin—"

His papier-mâché shoulders trembled under her fingers.

"You get hell outa heah!" he repeated, his voice rising
plaintively. "You damn fool, you listen Sin and get outa
heah now Saul dead. He laise plenty hell too soon!"

It was strangely frightening in that room clammy with
the presence of death, with the face of the dead man thinly
smiling in the glow of the setting sun.

2

At the sound of voices in the hall all expression drained from the face of the old Chinaman. He turned away from Helen and stood facing the bed. She recognized Nick Baron's voice, heard him say, "Easy does it."

She opened the door. Nick and Jeff Oliphant had set down her trunk in her room. They came to her quickly, Jeff pausing at her side, Nick going to the head of the bed. He drew the sheet over the pillows.

"When did you last see him?" he asked Sin.

"He sleep houah ago."

Nick Baron opened the medicine box. It was empty. He said to Sin, "I thought you carried these with you?"

"Godmighty!" the old man burst out irascibly. "Saftanoon he say he wait so long all leddy safe bet he wait while longa! Why'n hell not?" he demanded reasonably.

Jeff had turned and was looking at Helen. Her coppery hair and her red lips accented the pallor of her face.

"He's been on the point of death for several days," he said. "In great pain. This is really a merciful release."

But that, they all knew, did not answer Sin's question. There was no answer unless his purpose in waiting had been accomplished once it was too late for the news of his death to cause her to turn back. She pushed herself away from the doorframe against which she was leaning

and crossed the hall to her room. The sound of voices in
the hall, of footsteps coming and going to Saul Baron's
bedroom, had stopped by the time she had her clothes unpacked and the cosmetics from her dressing case spread on
top of the bureau. The sun had nearly left the earth. Only
the heads of the Two Saints were touched with light above
the darkening mountain.

Nick Baron was in his room changing to a dark suit.

"You ought at least to put on a black tie," he told Jeff.
"Have some consideration for her feelings. She's just a
sweet tender little thing who'd jump if you as much as set
off a blast of dynamite under her."

Jeff said, "Parsons must have heard us coming."

"Of course he heard us coming. He just didn't give a
damn."

"You think that's all?"

"It was nearly enough."

Jeff did not smile. "What do you think about tonight?"
he asked.

Nick sat down on the edge of the bed to change his golf
shoes for a black pair. He said, "I think I'll have a couple
of Jay's cocktails, a good meal in charming company and
then a little stroll under the stars. She's the passionate
type. Hate you one minute, love you the next!"

Jeff had a look of dogged patience. "Then you're not
expecting any trouble tonight?" he persisted.

"No," Nick said, "I don't think so. After all she's been
through she's going to crave a little emotional relaxation."

"Oh, the hell with it."

Jeff jerked open the door but, struck by the silence in the
hall, did not slam it. He went to the stairway in the middle of the hall. Below, in the lounge, Jay Warren Cole was
standing with his back to the fireplace talking with George
Sears and Harry McIntyre. He quickly coughed when he
caught sight of Jeff Oliphant coming down the stairs.

"Sylvia, the dear child, has taken a Manhattan up to Miss Farr," he announced. "I hope she can persuade her to join us. To be alone at such a time . . ." He gently shook his head.

He's missed his vocation, Jeff thought. He's such a dead ringer for an undertaker you can smell the lilies.

"Yes," he said, in reply. "Good idea. Yes."

He went to the tray of drinks, poured a cocktail, and looked out of a window until Sylvia and Helen came down the stairs. Dark and fair, he thought they looked well together. Cole took Helen in hand and solicitously conducted her to a chair in front of the fire. Sylvia followed more slowly, silken legs flowing beneath the thin drapery of her skirt, the firm, full curves of her breasts molded by her turquoise sweater. Jeff intercepted her.

"Your glass looks a little peaked," he said.

"Definitely anaemic," she agreed, setting it down for him to refill.

They both spoke in an undertone, their attention on what her father was saying to Helen Farr. But, sensibly, he was letting his commiserative manner speak for itself and was avoiding any reference to Saul Baron. Since he had instructed Sylvia to inform her of the funeral arrangements, that an undertaker would be brought out from Sasoon the first thing in the morning, he was at liberty to confine his comments to the weather. The quick change of temperature at sundown, he was explaining, was caused by the high altitude, and the cold air flowing down the mountain made even the desert cool at night. . . . Sylvia took a sip from her glass.

"Where's Nick?" she asked.

"In his room."

Her amber eyes studied Jeff over the rim of her glass as he poured himself another drink. He probably thought that he had perfectly concealed his jealousy by speaking

in a determinedly toneless voice and keeping a petrified
wood expression on his blunt face.

Captain McIntyre, drinking Scotch and soda without
ice, had carried the weather report from Arizona to British
New Guiana. He paused hopefully when Sylvia and Jeff
sat down, but when neither of them had anything to say,
his clipped voice monotonously went on with it, jerking
upward at the end of his sentences and leaving behind
him a trail of decapitated words hanging from the trees of
the tropical colony. George Sears sat and gazed at the fire
like a man alone, periodically raising a tumbler of rye and
water to his straight lips, the shadow of the glass flicker-
ing over the hard planes of his pock-marked face.

Helen's eyes followed Sin as he shuffled through the
lounge and adjoining dining room, lighting kerosene
lamps, then shifted to Nick Baron as he came down the
stairs. He had changed to a dark suit and a black necktie.
The thing that impressed her was that he had thought to
include a black four-in-hand in his wardrobe. That was
forethought to a degree not for the squeamish. As he surveyed the group at the fireplace she saw his eyes pause
with Sylvia and Jeff on their Mission sofa. It occurred to
her that Sylvia had sat down on the middle cushion to re-
serve a place beside her for Nick. Instead, with a sociable
smile, he took a chair beside her own.

Helen found that she and Sylvia were looking into each
other's eyes. Sylvia quickly smiled and said what was obviously the first thing to come into her mind.

"Is this your first trip West?" she asked.

Helen also smiled. "I left San Francisco when I was four."

Nick Baron said, "I was fourteen when I last was out
here. It was a swell time for a kid from Philly," he added
with a remembering smile. "The *pièce de résistance* was a
three-day prospecting trip with Billy Bedrock. Very close
to heaven, that. You've heard of Billy, I hope?"

"I think I remember the name," Helen said, and a thought went back to a little girl who, fascinated by something in the sound of it, had named her every doll Billy Bedrock. There had been Billy Bedrock Mary, and Billy Bedrock Goldilocks. . . .

"You'll enjoy meeting him," Nick was assuring her. "Quite a character! You've a treat in store if you've never heard the story of how Dead Finger Fault got its name. Billy was the discoverer of the mine, you know. Though Mr. Parsons has been disputing that for some twenty-five years, hasn't he, Jay?"

A strip of adhesive tape was like a white scar on Cole's face. It was a moment before he replied and in that moment Helen was aware of the tension in the silence of every person at the fireplace, a semi-circle of tense, unsmiling faces and Nick Baron smiling and at ease awaiting Cole's reply.

Cole said smoothly, "Billy staked the first claim."

"At any rate it's the one Uncle Saul bought," Nick told her. "And then he got down to the serious business of mining the stockholders." Leaning back in the chair, he met with a smiling stare the eyes of the three men who had been Saul Baron's partners. "Not counting the rake-off on the million or two that was spent here," he said, "about how much, just at a rough guess, would you say you'd taken away from the suckers?"

George Sears said, "I don't think that's what you want to know. I think you want to know how much of it Saul finally got away with."

Nick Baron nodded. "I'll admit that's more to the point." His smile became more pronounced, the lower lip more boldly protuberant. "But what I'd really like to know," he said, "is who is now going to get away with it?"

Sin shuffled in from the dining room.

"Come get glub."

It was an awkwardly silent dinner. As soon as they rose
from the table Helen made her excuses and went to her
room. She took from her suitcase a cabinet photograph
that Saul Baron had sent to her just before, as she now
knew, he had been sentenced to prison. Now she saw in his
face the same mocking boldness she had seen in Nick Baron's when he had stripped the three men at the fireplace
of any pretense to respectability that they might otherwise
have maintained in front of her. Whatever his purpose, it
had been cruel to do it in front of Sylvia Cole. Nicholas
Baron, Saul Baron. There was ruthless force in the face
that looked out at her from the past, the past in which her
father had been driven to suicide. And, undeniably, there
was something magnetic, that attracted unwillingly. Saul
Baron, Nick Baron. . . .

An hour later found her nerves too much on edge to
sit longer in the room and she shrank from facing any one
else. She left the lodge by the outside stairs at her end of
the hall. The sky was cloudless, moonless and amazing
with stars. Walking down the road it seemed out of the
world to see stars in the sky below the level of her feet.
She carried her own visible world with her, a circle that
moved with her, its circumference a few yards in front and
trailing a few yards behind through the silence and peace
of the night.

The dark bulk of the stampmill was the first thing to
remind her that she had walked farther than she had realized. Intending to turn back after making a circuit of the
mill on its narrow shelf above the bed of the gulch, she
was halfway around it when she heard the sound of voices.
The voices faded, then became more distinct, as though
two men, pacing up and down, were approaching the corner a few yards ahead of her.

". . . Damned fools to trust him alive or dead."

"There's well over a quarter of a million here, cash in hand. I'd trust the devil himself to get my hands . . ."

Turning hastily, her one thought not to be discovered, she stepped too near the edge and started a small slide of stones that sounded loudly to her ears, but there was no sound of alarm behind her and she quickly and quietly retraced her steps. As she rounded the corner of the mill to turn to the road she ran into a man's arms. She tried to jump back from him but found herself held in a firm grasp.

Nick Baron was smiling at her.

"Careful," he warned. "It's a thirty-foot drop to the bed of the gulch." When she turned and looked down at the thin darkness behind her she stopped trying to pull away from him. "It's really dangerous for you to run around here at night without a guide," he told her. "That's why you must thank me for following you."

Helen said, "Thank you kindly, sir. Or *did* mother tell me to thank men who follow—?"

They laughed, walked back up the road.

She did not believe that he had followed her from the lodge, although it was possible because she had not recognized the voices of the two men in the few words only indistinctly heard. She did not at that moment particularly care one way or the other. The thing that mattered was that she was no longer alone. She had been frightened and the worst of it had been the unreasoning fear that can come to one alone in the night; and now she was no longer alone.

Her first sense of mere relief became more a sense of companionship as they slowly went up the road together through the night. Outside the little circle of their companionship, the smile and steadying touch of his hand on her arm when she stumbled on a rock, she was conscious of the loneliness of the surrounding solitude, as wide as the night, as high as the stars. They walked side by side to the foot of the outside stairway. When she turned to say goodnight he kissed her.

Helen went up the stairs without speaking and without a backward glance. The thing that bitterly annoyed her was not that he had caught her by surprise, for he had not, but that he had known that he had not. As she stepped within the hall she was brought to a quick stop. A cigarette had been rubbed underfoot, but hurriedly, a coal of fire still glowing on the floor. Some one had stood in the doorway and had seen. . . .

It was suddenly of no importance. After a short escape she was again in the house where Saul Baron lay dead, and smiling as at some secret expectation. She left the door of her room wide open until she had lit her lamp. There was no key in the door. She propped the back of a chair under the doorknob. But she was not disturbed, even by mice, before she awoke late the following morning.

When she went downstairs for breakfast she learned from Sin that Nick Baron had driven Sylvia Cole and her father and George Sears to town. Sin was fussily anxious to make her breakfast a success but aside from his pampering service he was morose and reticent. She was glumly sipping her last cup of coffee when Jeff Oliphant came to the table.

"I wonder if you wouldn't like to get out of here for a while?" he asked. "We might take a walk around the mine."

"For a few kind words," Helen told him, "I'd follow you to the ends of the earth."

As they walked down the road Harry McIntyre watched them from the vantage point of his chair on the terrace in front of the lodge. He watched them turn off on the shaft to Gold Pocket claim and stand at the collar dropping rocks to splash in the green-scummed water that came to within twenty feet of the top. He watched them cross the bed of the gulch near the stampmill and follow the line of the conveyor towers up to the great tunnel on Sourdough.

He rose and went in the lodge. He went quickly up-stairs. As he started to enter Helen Farr's bedroom he was met by Sin coming out of its doorway. He was carrying her handbag. He held it up.

"Full plivate lettas and dough," he informed. "You can go in now."

Harry McIntyre spoke in a dangerously quiet tone. "God damn your insolence," he said. "Any more of it and I'll kick your yellow hide downstairs and up again."

Sin blinked at him. "You get too damn flesh, Hossy-Face," he prophesied, "you get damn bad belly ache when you eat."

Harry passed his hand over his head. He said resign-edly, "You haven't changed much in all these years, have you?"

"Change?" Sin spat out the word. "Same all time damn mean yellow-belly Chink. Maybe you change? Same all time small fly clook." His wizened face crinkled into a crepe-paper grin. "Maybe you like ask Saul him change?"

Harry McIntyre turned quickly from that grin. When he resumed his chair on the terrace in front of the lodge he saw doll-size figures sitting on the edge of the terrace across the gulch that was the dump of Sourdough tunnel.

"Cigarette?"

Helen shook her head, brushing back a wind-blown wisp of the sunlight and copper that was her hair.

"I think I'll catch my breath first!" she said. "My head's singing, my heart's pounding and my knees are still wab-bling—it's been a lovely walk!"

Jeff looked at her critically. "I'd say it was just what the doctor ordered," he decided. "Better color, increased animation, a less haunted look," he concluded.

"It's really been swell. I'll never regret a minute of having followed you to this—" with a quick, flat-handed gesture she indicated the mountain falling away into the distant desert and the foreground of the abandoned mine on the sides of the ravine—"this ends of the earth." Then, as she gazed across the gulch at the lodge, he saw her eyes become somber. "But we come back where we started, don't we?" she asked with a wan smile. She glanced aside at him. "You didn't bring me up here to look at the view."

Jeff came straight to the point. "There's a strongly held idea here that Uncle Saul may have left you the lion's share," he said. "If it turns out that way, watch your step."

Helen shook her head. "I'm the last. . . . You can rest assured that he hasn't favored me over you or your cousin," she concluded.

Jeff smiled briefly. "Over his own flesh and blood, you mean? Family tradition has it," he went on reflectively, "that my father had a standing promise to knock Uncle Saul down on sight for having eased my mother out of her share of their inheritance from their grandparents. As to Nick—when he was out here as a boy he was with his father, who had invested some money in the mine. The up-shot of that family reunion was that my Uncle John swore that he'd be pleased to forget that he had a brother who was a damned unblushing swindler." He shook his head. "Uncle Saul's family feeling," he said, "was a fine, cordial hate."

"There must be some one," Helen said. "There must be some one whom he loved."

Jeff shrugged. "There's Cole and Sears and McIntyre," he said. "Saul double-crossed them out of their share of what had been swindled from the stockholders and they struck back by turning state's evidence and sending him to prison. The other beneficiary is our neighbor, Mr. Parsons, whom Saul cheated out of the mine to begin with,

and who's been waging guerrilla war against Dead Finger
ever since. Yesterday was a mild sample. You see how it
is," he concluded. "If it weren't for you we'd be the oddest
lot of beneficiaries ever collected. You're the only one he
never hated."

There was a pinched look to Helen's face.

"Then," she said, "I guess we're the oddest lot ever
collected." She knew, now, the thing she had been unable to read between the lines of his last letter. . . . *Your
mother never suspected my betrayed of Frederick, but there
was the cruel justice of the following years when it was only
your childish jealousy of me, amounting to hatred, that kept
Elizabeth from marrying me. My life would have been very
different had she done so because I would have been a different man.* . . . She knew, now, that the thing that she had
sensed between those lines was hatred. She knew, now,
that he had reached out for her through all the years between not in love but in hatred.

"I'm scared green," she said. "I can't say I know from
experience how it feels to feel you're in a trap, but that's
the way I feel."

"You'll have to admit it's good bait," said Jeff thoughtfully. "Over a quarter of a million, cash in hand."

Helen had heard those words, the exact phrase, before.
It repeated itself in her mind late that afternoon when she
was one of the seven who sat expectantly at the dining-
room table in the lodge. It had been only a few minutes
before that those who had gone to town in the morning
had returned with Willet Price as an additional passenger,
and they had picked up Mr. Parsons when they had come
by his drift above the road. It had been only something
over an hour since a hearse had driven down the mountain
carrying the body of Saul Baron. But the haste in which
they were assembled to receive their legacies was simply in
compliance with his instructions to Willet Price.

Helen was seated at the foot of the table. At her right
sat Mr. Parsons. She saw a hunched little man with a mat
of gray hair and a stubble of gray beard bristling on his
crookedly outthrust jaw. From deeply sunken eyes he glared
with open hatred at every one else in the room. They were
facing Willet Price, who stood at the head of the table
with Sin a few feet behind him. They watched the gray-
haired lawyer take an envelope from his coat pocket and
unhurriedly open it and remove a sheet of notepaper.

"This was left in the drawer of Saul's bedside table," he
said. "Sin gave it to Mr. Nicholas Baron and Mr. Cole and
Mr. Sears, who brought it to me today." He lowered his
cold eyes to the sheet of paper and read aloud in his dry,
distasteful tone:

"*'Dear Will: As my old friend, not my lawyer, I ask you to
go to Dead Finger as soon as you receive this and see that certain private communications that I have left with Sin reach
the proper hands. In this way I think every one can avoid any
legal vexations. Thank you, Will, for this last service, Saul.'*

"There's a postscript," he added.

"*'To avoid misunderstanding between them, I wish you
would tell them that my only request in return for what I
have given is for them to make an open comparison of what
they have received and I think all must agree that I have
made a fair and impartial distribution. In that belief, I die
in peace.'*"

His voice stopped. The paper made a dry rustling sound
as he refolded it and put it back in the envelope. Sin shuffled forward and set a leather briefcase on the table. It was
closed with a padlock.

"Have you a key?" Willet Price asked.

There was a ring of metal on the table, startlingly loud
in the utter silence, and they stared at a key that had been
beaten into a thin wafer.

Sin said, "He gimme key and say pound 'em up. When I bling 'em back he gimme bliefcase. Say keep bliefcase and mouth shut 'til he dead. I got knife now."

He produced it from somewhere, a long razor-edged knife which he handed to Willet Price.

The lawyer began sawing at the heavy leather of the briefcase. The strain was intolerable. Wresting her eyes away, Helen Farr looked at the faces of those at the table. Each was hard with calculation as they gazed fixedly at the briefcase. Over a quarter of a million. How much over a quarter of a million? Three hundred thousand? Four? And my share, cash in hand . . .

A slight movement from Nick Barton, who was sitting to her left, caught her eye. He had unbuttoned his coat. She saw projecting from under the belt of his trousers the blue-steel butt of an automatic.

Her eyes returned to the head of the table as Willet Price put aside the knife and opened the briefcase. He took out, one after the other, seven manila envelopes that were about ten by twelve inches in size. Names were written on them. He slowly walked around the table placing an envelope in front of each person. When he stood again at the head of the table the seven envelopes still lay untouched where he had placed them.

"In view of Saul's wishes . . ." he said.

Helen's fingers fumbled with the string wound around a tab that closed the flap of the envelope. At last it was open. She drew out a mounted studio photograph of Saul Baron. It was inscribed:

To help you remember—Saul Baron.

There was nothing else in the envelope. The photograph was her complete inheritance. She looked around the table. They all had them. From seven identical photographs Saul Baron smiled at them.

3

Harry McIntyre was the first to speak.

"What use is the money to Saul now that he's dead?" he asked very calmly, very reasonably. "Why not hand it over? His letter made it seem quite reasonable. That's why I came flying here all the way from Minas Geraes," he explained, and his voice was higher. "To get this," he cried, turning his eyes to the photograph that lay face-up on the table in front of him. "To get this!" He beat his fist against the photograph.

George Sears rose, upsetting his chair, and wrenched the briefcase from Willet Price's hands. He looked in it and then with a jerk of his wrist flung it across the room. He took a step towards Sin.

"Are you holding out?" he asked.

Helen had not seen Sin repossess the butcher knife with which the heavy leather of the briefcase had been sliced apart, but she now saw that he was holding it in his hand and his hand at his waist. His beady eyes were running speculatively over George Sears's abdomen.

Jay Warren Cole raised a placating hand. "No, Red," he said. "No. He's not holding out. Saul left us nothing else. Nothing to spoil this." His round face was the pink-tinged white of suet but he was forcing a smile. "We know what he could have left us," he continued, his smile twitching.

"He knows that we know. That, I should say, is the cream of the jest." He looked at the photograph lying in front of him. "He must be laughing at us in hell."

A high, cackling laugh broke from Mr. Parsons. He scrambled to his feet clutching his grimy hat in one hand, his copy of the photograph in the other.

"Saul's jackassed ye!" he yelled at them. "By God, he's jackassed ye!" He waved the photograph at them. "All they's good's to spit at—an' ye don't even chaw, none of ye!"

He laughed again as he backed towards the door, and the girlish giggle sounded odd coming from his mouth with its brown drool of tobacco juice in the gray stubble of his beard. In the doorway he came to a stop and with a full-armed sweep of his hand flung the photograph on the floor at his feet. It landed face up. He spat at it, making a hit with a squirt of tobacco juice, and then picked it up and swaggered out of the lodge.

Helen saw Nick button his coat.

"Over a quarter of a million, cash in hand," he said. He snapped his fingers. "Easy come, easy go."

Only Sylvia's expression as she stood behind her father's chair seemed one of relief, thankful relief. Helen rose, facing Willet Price.

"When is the funeral?" she asked tonelessly.

"The day after tomorrow."

"I may stay here until then?"

"Stay long damn please," Sin spoke up harshly. "I boss this dump." No one contradicted him.

Helen turned from the table and went to her room. On top of her bureau Saul Baron smiled at her from a photograph that was inscribed, "To help you remember—your Uncle Saul." She had stood it on the bureau before going downstairs to receive her legacy. His smile mocked her from the duplicate that she held in her hand. "To help you remember—Saul Baron." She opened a bureau drawer and slipped it inside. She closed the drawer.

It's only shock, she told herself. You haven't really been run over by a truck. No bones broken. Just pick yourself up and dust yourself off.

That seemed to be the general idea when she rejoined the others for a cocktail before dinner. No one mentioned anything having anything to do with Dead Finger Fault. Even Willet Price, who was staying the night, seemed to feel that what had happened needed no rubbing in. It was not much after ten o'clock when they went to their rooms.

It was midnight when Helen left her room. She had got up too late that morning to get to sleep and she was hungry. The dark hall stopped her for a moment. As she stood in her doorway she thought she heard another door cautiously opened. She turned back for her lamp on the bureau. She did not see any doors ajar when she went down the hall carrying the lamp. She reminded herself that all houses are full of "bumps in the night" when you are the only person awake.

The kitchen was a disappointment. The only refrigerator that she could find was an electric one that had not been used since the power plant at the mine had been shut down. The best that she could scrape up was a pan of cold biscuits and a jar of jam. She was, slowly, finishing her sixth biscuit when there was the crunch of a footstep outside the open doorway. Nick Baron came in carrying a lantern and a basket in one hand and a platter in the other.

He looked at her biscuits and jam. "The icebox is kept in a little tunnel just outside," he explained. "Cooler."

Helen looked at the half of a baked ham on the platter and watched him unload the basket. There were four bottles of beer, a several-pound wedge of Swiss cheese, a half bottle of ripe olives and a wedge of Roquefort in tinfoil.

"I wish you'd come four or five biscuits ago," she said, bitterly.

"What about an olive on Swiss?"

"That," she admitted, "will be about my limit."

Nick grinned when he looked at her mouth. She knew that there was a smudge of blackberry jam at the corners of her lips because she was cleaning it off with the point of her tongue.

"That little-girl-in-the-pantry look," he said, "is quite piquant with your dressing gown."

He looked at the sophisticated cut of her dressing gown. When he got around to her face again Helen saw that he was seeing the shape of her lips and the color of her hair and that her eyes were something to look into as well as for her to look out of.

"I don't think I ever said some of the ungallant things I said to you," he decided. "It's against human nature. My nature's very human," he added.

"Oh, I knew you didn't really dislike me, Nick," Helen assured him. "I knew it was only because you were afraid he'd leave me something and there'd be that much less for you." She gave him a blackberry grin. "That's was why I couldn't resist making you kiss me last night," she explained. "You'd been trying so hard to make me afraid of you!"

It was a profound satisfaction to see how little he enjoyed that view of himself. That was the one comforting thing about vain men, they had as many Achilles' heels as a centipede. Protesting that she couldn't eat another bite, Helen returned to her room feeling very good.

She found the photograph of Saul Baron that she had left standing on the bureau torn up and thrown on the floor. The half-dozen pieces, some face up and others with the cardboard backing turned up, were strewn from the bureau nearly to the doorway in which she stood, the lamp wavering in her hand.

When she had the door closed behind her and a chair propped under the doorknob a quick inspection of the drawers of her bureau showed that her room had not been searched. She gathered up the scattered fragments of the photograph and sitting down on the edge of the bed spread them out beside her. As she pieced them together she tried mentally to piece together the picture of what had happened.

Some one must have waited until she was downstairs and then come to her room solely for the purpose of finding Saul Baron's photograph to tear it up in a rage and throw it on the floor. That was what had happened and it was incredible.

Staring at the jagged jigsaw, it occurred to her that no one at the lodge had seen that copy of the photograph before she had received the other as her legacy. Not knowing she had a duplicate, the person who had found it on top of her bureau had believed it was the one which Saul Baron had bequeathed to her. What had happened was incredible unless that person had some sane but secret reason for tearing up the particular copy that was her legacy.

Helen went to the bureau and took the other photograph out of the drawer. She tried to tear it in two. The mat broke easily for an inch from the edge and then was stopped by a sheet of linen. The mat had been sliced apart, the sheet of linen laid flat on one half, and the mat glued back together around the edges only. The sheet of white linen, glazed as though cut from a window-shade, was about six by nine inches in size. One side was black with single-spaced typewriting. She spread it on top of the bureau directly under the lamplight and read:

Beginning at SE corner monument of Gold Pocket claim the line from same to NW corner monument is the base line 0-360°. The line from last established point to preceding point is new base line for angle departure to next. Any three of the Charts. Example: with Charts 1, 4, and 7:

1st HALF

1. No. 1 gives Starting Direction. Locate point.
2. No. 1 " Key Letter to No. 4.
3. No. 4 " Key Direction. Locate point.
4. No. 4 " Key Letter to No. 7.
5. No. 7 " Key Direction. Locate point.

2nd HALF

Continue from above but reverse sequence of Charts, i.e.: 7, 4, 1.
THIS IS CHART No. 2.
STARTING DIRECTION: 1440 ft. 135°

1st HALF: Key Letter G for No. 3
       "   "   J " No. 4
       "   "   H " No. 5
       "   "   D " No. 6
       "   "   A " No. 7

2nd Half: "   "   R " No. 1

OWN KEY LETTERS

1st HALF	2nd HALF
A — 1468 ft. 315°	A — 1380 ft. 135°
B — 913 ft. 45	B — 1090 ft. 270
D — 1060 ft. 135	C — 1272 ft. 270

E — 880 ft. 180	D — 874 ft. 45
G — 1784 ft. 152	H — 848 ft. 225
H — 1240 ft 180	I — 1250 ft. 90
K — 1294 ft. 315	K — 1150 ft. 180
M — 1160 ft. 225	N — 980 ft. 45
N — 628 ft. 90	O — 1438 ft. 250
O — 970 ft. 270	P — 1160 ft. 270
Q — 1280 ft. 270	Q — 1400 ft. 90
R — 1056 ft. 45	R — 950 ft. 90
T — 1787 ft. 315	S — 857 ft. 217
U — 1258 ft. 135	T — 1472 ft. 122
W — 1180 ft. 270	V — 1203 ft. 196

The chart ended with the two parallel columns of letters and figures.

Helen was staring at it with the realization that she was reading directions to the place where Saul Baron had cached his fortune when some one tapped at the door. She hastily closed the photograph and the chart in the bureau drawer. When she went to the door she left the chair propped under the knob.

"Yes?"

"It's I, Helen." It was Sylvia's voice.

Helen opened the door reluctantly. Sylvia was in a Chinese yellow housecoat that was becoming to her dark beauty. She was, as usual, very calm and gave the impression of being very sure of herself.

"I saw your light down here when I looked out my window a moment ago," she explained.

"I haven't been sleepy."

"Miserable, isn't it? I've been restless too. I got up to take a sleeping tablet and when I saw your light I wondered if you wouldn't like one?"

"That's awfully nice of you! But I don't think I need one."

Sylvia offered a small bottle. "They're very good."

"Thanks, but I never take them."

Helen saw Sylvia looking towards the bed. She had forgotten to put away the pieces of the torn photograph that she had fitted together. Sylvia glanced at her.

Helen said. "A fit of temper."

"I don't wonder!" Sylvia smiled kindly but firmly. "Take one of these and you'll feel ever so much better after a good night's sleep."

"Thanks so much, but I have a prejudice against them. Silly, I guess! But I'd prefer not to."

"But don't you think it's really dangerous?" Sylvia asked persuasively. "I mean to go on in such a state of nerves, not to get enough sleep."

Helen turned and went to the window. A cut had been made in the side of the ridge for the terrace on which the lodge stood. The rear windows of the second floor were tan like first-floor windows and the ridge went on up so sharply that any one standing even some distance from the window could have looked down into her room and could not have failed to have seen her when she had removed the chart from the photograph. It also would not be too difficult for any one to climb in her window. In that case it might be safer for her to be in a drugged sleep than to awaken. Was that what she was being told? She faced Sylvia.

"I must see your father," she said. "Will you call him for me, ask him to come here with you?"

After a long moment Sylvia said, "If you wish."

Helen stood in the doorway of her bedroom while Sylvia walked down the hall. The only light was from the lamp on the bureau behind her and from the open doorway of Sylvia's bedroom at the far end of the hall. The door of Cole's bedroom was directly opposite Sylvia's own. Sylvia tapped on the door and then entered, closing it behind her.

Helen quickly stepped into the hall. To surround Saul Baron's sick-room with quiet the earlier arrivals had been billeted at the far end. Next to her own corner room was one of the baths and then a vacant room. Opposite her room was the one Saul Baron had occupied and then another vacant room between it and Jeff Oliphant's bedroom. She had no intention of confiding her discovery to Jay Warren Cole while alone with him and Sylvia in her isolated bedroom.

She ran to Jeff's door. She did not want to rouse Sears or McIntyre and rapped gently. There was no reply. In desperation she opened the door and entered the room. By the thin darkness of the starlit night outside the window she was, after an instant, able to locate the bed. She heard a door open in the hall. Hastening to the side of the bed her foot struck against a yielding mass on the floor and she fell forward onto the bed. In the same instant that her outspread arms told her that the bed was empty she realized that she had stumbled over a body.

As Helen pushed herself back from the bed and knelt on the floor she was aware that lamplight was advancing along one wall of the room from the open doorway. Jeff was stretched out at the side of the bed with the bed covers pulled down around him as if he had fallen out of bed. He was lying on his face. She was suddenly aware that lamplight was shining full upon her as she knelt, trembling, staring at the inert figure in front of her.

She turned her head as Jay Warren Cole, hastened through the doorway followed by Sylvia. He stopped short two or three steps within the room, holding the lamp high, a startled fat man in a wine dressing gown and red-striped pajamas. At a gesture from him Sylvia closed the door. She remained standing with her back to the door, a dimly seen figure in Chinese yellow, her face obscure except for her almond eyes.

Still kneeling on the floor, Helen watched Cole set the lamp on a bedside table. Kneeling beside her, he rolled Jeff over on his back. A moan came from the unconscious man. Cole turned his round face towards the door. There were patches of white in his florid complexion.

"Whisky, my dear," he said. "You'll find some in my room."

Sylvia slipped out the door.

Jeff moaned, rolled his head. Cole pulled a pillow from the bed and worked it behind the other man's shoulders,

"A wet towel, my dear," he said to Helen.

There was a washbasin in a corner of each bedroom.

The water was siphoned from a well higher up the side of the mountain and flowed strong and icy cold. Helen sopped a towel. Cole bathed Jeff's face, put the towel to the back of his neck. Jeff opened his eyes.

"Quiet, my dear young friend. Quiet."

Sylvia returned with a bottle of rye and Cole held it to Jeff's lips. Jeff coughed, pushed himself up to a sitting position, and then taking the bottle of rye in his own hand helped himself to it.

Cole said, "Can you tell us what happened?"

Jeff lowered the bottle. "Why not?" he asked.

Cole said, "I mean do you feel well enough?"

Jeff's eyes shifted to Helen and Sylvia. He picked up a package of cigarettes lying on the floor under the bedside table. The table was standing askew from the wall. Matches were scattered over its top and on the floor. He picked up one and lit a cigarette.

He said, "It looks like I fell out of bed and hit my head on the table." He gave Helen a stiff smile. "Sorry if I bounced so hard that I woke you up."

Helen wondered how, if he had been unconscious, he knew that she had been the first person in the room.

Jeff put his arms along the bed behind him and heaved himself up to a sitting position on the edge of the bed. His expression was that of a man just arising with a bad hangover. He saw that Helen was looking at his bureau. The drawers were irregularly open and articles of clothing were hanging over the edges.

"Your copy of the photograph!" she exclaimed. "Where were you keeping it?"

"I wasn't," Jeff told her. "I tossed it out the window before I turned in. It's out there somewhere. Why?"

Helen went quickly to the door.

"Please wait!"

There was no one in the hall. She drew the door shut behind her and ran for the open doorway of her own bedroom. She found the chart and the photograph where she had left them in the bureau drawer. Returning to Jeff's room, she stopped short with her hand on the doorknob. Nick was standing on the top step of the stairs from the lounge. When he saw that he was discovered he stepped straight ahead to his own door. His blatant delicacy in not noticing that she was paying a visit to Jeff's bedroom was given a double edge by the knowing leer that she saw on his face.

Helen said coldly, "If I may speak to you a moment?" She swung open the door as he turned. Nick looked past her at the arrested figures of the three people in the room. She said to him, "You'd better call Captain McIntyre and Mr. Sears. And I'd like for Mr. Price to be present. I've found how we can find the fortune we came here to get."

Ten minutes later they were gathered around the dining-room table. They did not need the drinks they had poured. They drank them and poured more while they laughed and talked. Saul Baron became an object of profane cordiality.

"The same old S. B.! It might have been years—"

"But that would have been perfect, Harry! Perfect. Five years from now, we're scattered over half the world. Only one or two of us have kept his damned photograph. One or . . ."

"Any three in sequence lowest to highest, then reverse."

"Miss Farr, for instance. She's looking at some old photographs. She picks up Saul's. In five years the glue has dried out The backing is split open. She finds the chart. Useless! Unless she can find two others, and . . ."

"Soda?"

"Thanks . . . that's enough!"

"You don't seem very joyous. Look at your father. He's joyous."

"Jeff. . . . Why don't you tell?"

"I'm afraid you wouldn't listen. If you'll promise to listen there's some very nice things I can—"

"Oh, my God!"

"I'm sorry. Honestly, I don't know who hit me."

"Why won't you tell?"

"At last she does manage to locate you and she tells you about the chart. But you've thrown your copy away!"

"When I think we might have left here cursing him for having brought us here for nothing, while in fact we'd be carrying away with us a full set of directions to a fortune!"

"God, how he must have laughed."

Helen walked out of the dining room. She went straight through the lounge to the door and out of the lodge. She went to the edge of the terrace, as far as she could away from the lodge. She sat down on a rustic bench at the edge of the terrace, her back to the lodge. She had been sitting there about two minutes when she heard the crunch of a footstep on the stone. Willet Price sat down beside her.

He was the only one whom she would not have resented following her. He had stood apart from the others, looking on with an expression of distaste as though he, too, had found the scene somewhat ghoulish. The laughing voices in the lodge were heard only faintly out here as meaningless wisps of sound in the clean night air, of no importance where a mountain was nothing in the night.

Beside her, Willet Price said, "In the heyday of the mine there was more to see. There was a night shift then, lights from the power plant." His dry voice added details: "Floodlights at Sourdough tunnel, on the conveyor towers, at the mill."

The darkness into which Helen was gazing faded. Directly opposite her above the void of the ravine the great rock terrace that was the dump of Sourdough tunnel was bright in light; diminutive dump cars ran from the mouth of the tunnel to the edge of the terrace and cascaded their loads of rock down its side while other cars carried their loads of ore to the conveyor line. Aerial skips swung on their cable in a path of light down the side of the ravine to the stampmill, bright in light, and pulsating the night with its thumping roar. . . .

Willet Price had said something else: "The lights of the trucks carrying the concentrate from the mill to the railroad."

Then she saw that too: the lights of trucks swinging out of sight around the curve below the stampmill, the lights of other trucks returning.

"At night? On that road?" she asked.

The dry voice beside her said that it had proved as safe as daytime transport. At night, on the worst curves, the beam of the headlights of an approaching car could be seen in time for the one coming up the mountain to draw off and stop in one of the numerous passing or turnaround niches that had been blasted out. She must have noticed them?

"Yes," Helen remembered. "We parked in one yesterday while Mr. Parsons blasted rocks over our heads."

"For twenty-five years," the lawyer said, "he's been brooding over the thought that he was cheated out of all this."

The irony of it sank in slowly as the lights of the past went out and there was only the darkness over the wreckage that lay abandoned in it.

"There's something frightening about this place," Helen said. "Mr. Parsons poisoning a lifetime over having been cheated out of nothing but a cheat. All the investors who were deluded into having such hopes in it only to be cheated out of their money and left without hope."

The dry voice beside her said, "But you expect the outcome to be different for you?"

She realized that this was why he had joined her, that this was what he had been leading up to. "You mean," she said, "that you do not think it will be?"

"You ought to be able to judge that for yourself, Miss Farr. Tonight two people became interested in the photographs. One of them very sensibly kept his mouth shut and began collecting them for himself. That he is not now in a position to find the fortune by himself and for himself is due only to the fact that he seems to have played in a run of remarkably bad luck. But the other person like a good little girl threw all the advantage of her discovery away."

"Simply because I must deal with swindlers I don't intend to become like them."

"Swindlers?" he picked up the word as if studying it. "Mr. Jeffery Oliphant," he said, "owns a small warehouse in a suburb of Chicago. While Mr. Nicholas Baron," he continued, "is connected with some financial house in Philadelphia."

"I can imagine what kind."

"Perhaps," his tone dismissed it as of no importance. "But you may be dangerously deluding yourself if you think you are dealing merely with 'swindlers.' When you think of 'swindlers' you think of sly tricksters who depend solely upon their wits to gain their ends. Instead, you might think of what happened to Mr. Oliphant tonight." To her surprise, there was anger in his voice. "This is a game for high stakes, Miss Farr. There is not a man in it who wants to divide the pot. If you sit in for a cut of it don't expect special treatment because of your sex or the sterling honesty of your character. You've no right to expect it and you won't get it. Understand that clearly before you start."

Nick spoke from the doorway of the lodge.

"Will you join us, Helen? We're just dealing the first round." He waited for her and Willet Price. "Red's worried about your scruples," he told her as they crossed the lounge to the dining room.

"I don't want any trouble later on," Sears explained. "And this nest egg of Saul's is something we're all going to have to keep very quiet about. Before we go any farther I must have your promise that, regardless of what you think about what I am going to tell you, you will keep it secret."

Harry McIntyre looked up from a map of the property that had been taken from where it had hung on the office wall and spread on the dining table.

"If not," he said, "you're simply out, and that's all there is to it."

Helen said, "I won't be a party to robbing any one. I'm not trying to read you a moral lesson," she added, Willet Price having rubbed her a little raw about her self-righteousness. "It's simply that I couldn't enjoy money if I knew I'd taken it from some person who had a better claim."

"Of course not, my dear child," Cole agreed heartily. "Of course not! But your fears are groundless. Completely groundless. There is no widow or orphaned child to haunt your enjoyment of your good fortune!"

No one contradicted him.

"Very well, then," Helen said. "You have my promise."

Sears came directly to the point. "We've good reason to believe that this nest egg of Saul's is gold," he said. "Minted gold. Saul took it from safe deposit boxes and cached it up here before he went to prison. He was in prison when the gold law was signed in 1933. He did not turn the gold in."

Helen appealed to Willet Price. "Just where does that leave us legally?"

Jay Warren Cole stepped between them. He chuckled and patted her shoulder.

"Let's settle this out of court, my dear!" He beamed upon her. "There's no need for us both to become involved in all the law's delays and vexations. When we find out how much your share amounts to I'll take it off your hands at its full minted value!"

George Sears said, "I want this clear. When we divide what we find you pay her off and she quietly goes about her business leaving us to attend to ours without interference. . . . Yes," he decided, "that ought to avoid trouble. That ought to satisfy everybody. It satisfies you, doesn't it?" he asked Helen.

She saw that Nick was smiling at her mockingly. She said through drawn lips, "Yes, I'm satisfied."

Captain McIntyre was nervously fidgeting with a protractor and a pair of dividers. "All right, then," he said, "let's get on with it. We can scale off one set of three charts and check ourselves with another three. Know where it is in a few minutes."

Willet Price spoke up of his own accord for the first time. "Not with that map," he said.

"What?"

"When Saul returned," he explained as if enjoying a dry joke, "he had me give him all the topographical survey

maps that had been left in my office. I happen to know that
he had Sin burn those maps before you people arrived."

Harry McIntyre cursed.

Jeff said, "I don't get it."

"This is a property map," McIntyre explained impatiently, indicating the gridiron of lines that marked the
boundaries of the score and more of claims that made up
the mine of Dead Finger Fault. "It has no contour lines."

Jeff said stubbornly, "I still don't get it."

McIntyre tapped his finger on the marked location of
the lodge and then on the tunnel of Sourdough.

"About how far apart would you say they are?" he asked.

"Eighteen inches."

Placing his hands on the edges of the map, McIntyre
drew them nearer together. The paper buckled into two
ridges with a hollow between.

"Now?" he asked.

"Nine inches."

"So that if you measured eighteen inches in an air line
you'd overshoot the mark, wouldn't you? That's our trouble. Since Saul worked out these charts on a topographical
map it means that the measurements he's given us aren't on
the flat but follow the contour of the ground."

"And with those maps destroyed," Sears said, "we'll
have to work it out on the ground. It is," he added, "going
to be a job."

Helen felt her heart sink as they discussed it. One thing
only was clear to her and that was that it was going to take
a long time. From the expression on Sylvia Cole's face she,
too, felt something close to panic at the thought of a prolonged stay at Dead Finger Fault under the tensions—and
the temptations—of a search for minted gold.

The discussion ended with the decision to go to Sasoon
in the morning for a surveyor's transit, tape and rod. They
would, of course, do their own surveying.

Nick was looking at his chart. "How do we line up?" he asked. "I'm number 7. Helen said she's number 2. You, Jeff?"

Jeff was number 4, Cole number 6, Sears number 3 and McIntyre number 5. Helen was not particularly interested in the numbers. The thing that interested her was that no one dropped his chart on the table, no one showed his chart to any one else.

When the list was completed Nick said, "So number 1 is Mr. Parsons."

They had forgotten Mr. Parsons. They looked at each other and then they looked at Helen. She understood the look. They were willing to keep on forgetting Mr. Parsons. She answered the look with finality.

"We'll tell Mr. Parsons in the morning," she said, and in the morning she was to wonder if Mr. Parsons might not still have been alive if she had not made him that promise.

4

Breakfast was at seven. No one had had more than three or four hours' uneasy sleep and the day's business was settled in a few grumbled words. Nick would drive Price to town. McIntyre would go along to get the surveying equipment. On their way they would stop at the tunnel and tell Mr. Parsons about the charts.

"If that will be satisfactory, Miss Farr?" Harry McIntyre asked the question but his resentment spoke for them all.

Helen said that it would be satisfactory. "Since Mr. Price is with you I don't think you'll forget to stop."

That ended conversation until Billy Bedrock came in and joined them at the table. He was a slender little white-haired man with the dashing mustache of the Old West. His leathery face was that of a gentle adventurer and his eyes had the look of squinting through the sunlight at far horizons. If all else since Helen Farr's arrival at Dead Finger had been different than her anticipations, Billy Bedrock was so like what she had pictured him to be that it was like meeting an old friend.

She expected him to start talking about gold nuggets but he did better than that. He showed her a plump little bottle containing nuggets ranging in size up to one as large as a lima bean.

"I picked that biggest fellow up last year," he told her.
"He was stuck in a crack on the bare bedrock of a wash I
was following along and he winked up at me as pretty as
you please. That's the way with gold. If it wants you to
find it you can't keep out of its way. Other times it just
keeps leading a man on."

He shook his head. "Even to his death sometimes,"
he said. "Was a time when this was bad Apache country,
none worse, and many a prospector was led on up here
to his death. Finds a color in a wash down in the foothills and says to himself, 'I can camp one night and turn
back tomorrow.' Then the next day the gold's showing up
real promising and he says the same thing to himself and
camps a second night. And the next day the gold keeps
leading him on."

It occurred to Helen that she had also camped there her
second night.

"He knows he's overstayed his time," Billy told her.
"He's seen Indian sign. He knows death is hanging around
up here too close for breathing. But he's close to a gold
strike, it looks like. Too close to leave it and save his skin.
So he says to himself, kind of under his breath, 'I'll camp
here just one more night and turn back tomorrow—sure!'
So he makes his camp a third time, maybe right where this
lodge is standing, and he goes to sleep thinking of the gold
he's going to find come morning—"

His gentle voice paused and he tilted his head to one side
as a deep detonation echoed over the mountain. It was the
sound of a dynamite blast. Mr. Parsons was early at work.

"But, come morning," Billy Bedrock picked up his
interrupted story, "he finds out kind of too late it's his last
day on earth."

"We can't listen to this all day," Harry McIntyre broke
in curtly. "We've more important matters to discuss. Private matters."

Helen was not surprised that one of them had interrupted the story, but the brutality of McIntyre's shut-up-and-get-out-of-here angered her. She rose from the table with Billy, who looked as if he had been kicked.

"Heaven help us," she said, "from an airing of the Captain's private affairs. At breakfast I can stand just so much."

Billy Bedrock asked respectfully, "Do you feel that way too, Miss?"

She looked at him with delighted surprise; given an ally he could strike a blow for himself. She decided that there was more than she had suspected behind those innocent eyes.

"When are you going to show me how to hunt for nuggets?" she asked, and added with bravado, "Indians or no Indians?"

It made him proud. "Why, Miss, I know a promising place I been saving right for this morning."

Sylvia said, "Since Helen's going to be running over the mountain I might as well ride in to town."

Nick said, "Fine."

Jeff pushed back his chair. "Can I get in on this prospecting?" he asked.

Helen felt sorry for him and annoyed with Sylvia for having hurt him, but pleased at the way the pairing-off had turned out. She felt at ease with Jeff. Both parties departed at about the same time, leaving Cole and Sears at the lodge. Billy said that the place he had in mind was over the ridge behind Sourdough. It was a half hour before they reached the top of the ridge.

Jeff said, "I wonder why the car's coming back?"

They watched it run up the road on the other side of the ravine from the stampmill to the lodge. Presently a lone figure stood at the edge of the terrace. An instant later there was the sound of three pistol shots.

"They must be signaling us to come back."

Billy had led them to the top of the ridge by a zig-zag path. They took a straight line going down, too busy keeping their footing to talk. The signal was repeated just before they came out on the dump of Sourdough tunnel where they were sighted from the terrace. The car turned around and went down the road. They met it at the stamp-mill. Nick was behind the wheel with Sears and Cole in the back seat. Their faces were stony.

"There's been an accident," Nick said. "A dynamite accident." He was looking at Billy Bedrock.

Helen did not instantly comprehend the full meaning of the words but she saw that Billy understood something that drained him of all spirit and left him looking old and ill.

"There was something we wanted to see Mr. Parsons about," Nick told him. "That's how we happened to stop at the drift. He wasn't there. There wasn't the muck of a blast. We went on back to his cabin. That's where it had happened."

Helen was holding tight to the side of the car. Nick glanced at her. "You'll find Sylvia at the lodge." She pushed herself back a step, stood rigid. Jeff got in the back seat with Cole and Sears. Billy put his hand on the door to the front seat.

Nick Baron said to him, "There's enough of us to take care of everything until I can get some one out from Sasoon. You'd better not go along, Billy. I know you were his friend. You don't want to see it."

"No," Billy said tonelessly. "No, I wouldn't like to have to see it." He dropped his hand from the door and turned away from them and slowly went down the trail beside the stampmill.

Nick started the car. Helen walked back up the road to the lodge. Sylvia was in the lounge drinking a highball. She looked as though she needed it.

"I went with them," she said woodenly.

Helen thought, *So you could have Nick help you over the trail.*

"It was a little rock cabin," Sylvia was telling her. "There's no roof left. One wall's blown away . . . level. Fragments of things . . . everywhere. I didn't go close, but I saw . . . in a tree . . ." She looked greenish.

Helen said contritely, "I didn't realize—they didn't tell me—"

"I wasn't close," Sylvia repeated. She said the words again as if by the repetition of the thought she were trying to push herself farther and farther away from what she had seen. She took a long drink, finishing her glass, poured another.

"Billy—has he gone with them?" she asked.

"Nick told him it wasn't necessary."

"That was thoughtful of Nick."

"Very," said Helen, her gorge rising. "Billy won't be in the way while they search for the photograph."

It was after one o'clock when Nick Baron returned from his trip to Sasoon. Cole, Sears, Jeff and McIntyre were riding with him. Only Harry McIntyre and Willet Price had accompanied him to town. Cole, Sears and Jeff had waited at Mr. Parsons' for those who had come from town to take charge of the remains of the dead man. Contrary to the custom of the country, those men were not, Nick said, coming to the lodge for lunch.

"They don't feel like eating lunch," he explained.

Harry McIntyre looked as though he did not feel like eating lunch. He poured himself two quick drinks before handing the bottle to Jeff. Sin came in with some more glasses, another bottle of whisky and some cracked ice. Sylvia stopped him at her chair and poured some more whisky into her highball. She had been drinking all morning. She was stone sober.

Helen said, "We'd rather know what happened than to go on imagining things."

Nick looked at her with one black eyebrow drawn up higher than the other. His hawk-nosed face had a disturbing expression, as though he was contemplating telling her things that she would not like to hear.

Jeff said, looking at Nick warningly, "There's not much to tell. It seems that these old prospectors usually keep their box of dynamite and detonation caps under their bunks."

"It's out of the way," George Sears explained quietly. "And it keeps the dynamite from freezing in the winter."

"He may have dropped the box of caps this morning," Jeff continued, "or dropped something on them."

Jay Warren Cole patted Helen's shoulder. "Accidents with explosives are a common sort of thing in a mining country, my dear," he assured her soothingly. "Very common! Very. It's almost the natural form of death for old prospectors."

Sylvia said from her chair, "Did you find the photograph?"

It brought an odd pause. One of the others might have answered her sooner except that Sylvia was looking steadily at her father. Cole at last accepted the fact that the question was addressed to him.

He shook his head. "If it were in the cabin it must have been blown to shreds."

"If it were?" Sylvia repeated.

Jeff said, "He may not have kept it. The way he was feeling about it when he left here he probably dropped it down a shaft to float around with the dead rats."

Nick said, "Rough on the rats."

Sylvia rose from her chair. "What are you trying to avoid telling us?" she asked.

Nick had stepped to the table to pour himself a drink. He said over his shoulder, "We'd feel more comfortable if the photo had been found." He finished pouring his drink.

"Do you mean that it was stolen?"

He studied his drink, took a sip. "We went to bed, or our bedrooms, around two o'clock last night," he replied. "It's only a twenty-minute walk to the cabin."

"But," Helen objected, "Mr. Parsons would have been there, and we know he was alive this morning."

Nick said, "Jeff fell out of his bed when he woke up in his room last night. Mr. Parsons may have fallen harder."

Helen forced out the words: "Do you mean he could have been murdered?"

"I'm told that the blast could have been set last night."

Captain McIntyre's narrow face was sharp and white. "We found a glop of candle tallow plastered against one of the walls—what was left of it," he said. "Embedded in it was a shred of burned fuse. It burns three feet per minute," he explained impatiently. "But a candle can be made into a time fuse by cutting a hole in it and putting the end of the fuse against the wick. The candle could have been lighted at any time last night and not burned down to the fuse until this morning—when we heard the blast at breakfast."

Jay Warren Cole raised a hand in protest. He made soothing motions in the air as if gently stroking a cat. "We don't want to exaggerate this," he pleaded. "It's merely a possibility. A mere mechanical possibility. There are a dozen other explanations!"

George Sears lowered a glass of whisky and water from his thin lips. "Of course there are," he said quietly. "That's why we didn't call the attention of any one from Sasoon to this one." He tilted the glass to his lips again.

Sylvia slowly walked straight ahead to the stairs and slowly mounted the stairs to her room. It was some two

hours later that Nick found her seated at her dressing
table, improvised from a bedside table and a mirror, made
feminine by the array of perfume bottles and cosmetics
upon it. He stood behind her, his hands on the back of
her chair, looking at her in the mirror. When she turned
her head and looked up into his face his hands slipped
from the back of the chair to her shoulders and he bent to
kiss her waiting lips. To his complete surprise she turned
her face to the mirror again and he was left with his lips
brushing the top of her hair. Of half a mind to tilt back
her head and finish what he had been invited to start, he
was too late for it to be spontaneous.

Sylvia said, "Fresh lip rouge might be awkward if any
one came to the door." It was a good out for them both.

He again stood with his hands on the back of the chair
looking at her in the mirror. Her smile was equivocal. He
wondered if her purpose had been to test how much he had
wanted to kiss her.

"I thought it was Helen when you rapped at the door,"
she continued smoothly.

"I don't know where she is," he said. "She's not in her
room."

Sylvia picked up a perfume bottle. "So this is just your
second port of call, Nick?" she asked, smiling.

"Business before pleasure."

Her fingers twisted at the ground-glass stopper of the
bottle. She said, "It oughtn't to be hard to persuade her to
leave—now."

"You think that I want to?"

Sylvia dabbed the glass stopper of the perfume bottle
against her hair. Her eyes caught his in the mirror. "I
think that with you, Nick, it will always be business before pleasure," she said, rising.

On leaving her room they met Jeff in the hall.

Nick said, "You make three of us. If we can find Helen we can have a game of bridge."

Jeff was looking thoughtfully at Sylvia. "All right by me," he agreed. "I think she's typing a letter in the office," he added. "I'll ask her if she wants to play."

Helen was through with typing the letter when Jeff entered the office. For some two hours past, the principal object of her activities had been to avoid every one at the lodge. She had not spoken with any one since Sylvia had slowly mounted the stairs from the lounge. No one, then, had had anything more to say. She had gone outdoors and sat on the terrace while the men were having lunch.

Before they rose from the table she went to her room. When restlessness drove her out again she took the stairs at the end of the hall. Nick and Harry were sitting on the terrace. She turned back under the stairway and entered the office through its outer door in the end of the lodge. The lounge was in the middle of the ground floor with the dining room and kitchen on one side and the office on the other.

The office was larger than the dining room and kitchen combined, because the quarters of Sin and his young helper were to the rear of those two rooms. It had once been divided into several offices by glass partitions, but in the years since the abandonment of the mine Sin had utilized the partitions for the growing of vegetables under glass and the winter protection of a fig tree. Draftsmen's tables and open cabinets were covered with the dust of neglected years. Two exceptions were a desk and chair beside a window near the living-room end of the office. There was a portable typewriter on the desk. In an open drawer was a sheaf of typewriter paper with an engraved letterhead: *Cole Investment Counsel Associates*. It was impressive. Helen put a sheet in the typewriter and began a letter to her Aunt Vicky.

She was on the third page when her attention was distracted by the sight of a white linen window shade lying on the floor. It was the only window shade that she had seen in the lodge. When she examined it she found that its edge had been cut with a pair of scissors. She nearly dropped it as the lounge door swung open.

Jeff looked apologetic. "Sorry I gave you a start," he said. "I could have knocked."

"Or seen my secretary for an appointment." Her white angora sweater with short puffed sleeves gave her a pert, airy look that was at odds with her smoldering mood. "But I'm afraid I'm not interested," she said, "unless you're selling life insurance."

Jeff sat down on a corner of the desk. He said, "As far as I know I haven't been trying to sell you anything."

"No," she admitted, thinking back, "that was unfair. You've let me go my own way without offering any suggestion or hints or threats."

"It isn't because I don't give a damn."

"Oh, I like you too," Helen assured him glibly. She pulled the sheet of paper out of the typewriter and picking up the other two began tearing the three together into small pieces.

"It was to my aunt," she explained, her gray eyes glancing up at him bright with temper. "A very dear person who might become uneasy if she were given too many lines to read between." She swept the scraps into her hand and rose from the desk. "It'll be safer to send a telegram."

Jeff said doubtfully, "In a small town, you know, a telegram's about as private as a postcard."

"Don't be worried," she snapped. "I'm only going to say, 'Uncle Saul typed directions to bullion on window shade Attending first funeral today Wish you were here Love Helen.'" She flung the scraps of paper on the floor.

"Or perhaps I should add, 'Second death possibly murder Secret Don't tell'?"

He said gravely, "You sound as if it'd be a relief to you to make it public?"

"What do you think?" she demanded fiercely. "When if I hadn't insisted that he be told he might still be alive! Do you think I feel like protecting you, any of you?"

Jeff stood facing her. "I don't think I'd let any one else here know how you feel," he said. "It might make them nervous about you." He did not belabor the point. "I came in to ask you to be a fourth at bridge," he remembered. "Sylvia and Nick are the others."

Her anger was not turned aside. "I'm sorry. I don't feel like pretending that nothing's happened."

The bridge game was under way with Harry McIntyre in her place when Helen left the lodge. She was on her way to make a call on Billy Bedrock. Since morning she had had in her mind the picture of him as he had turned from the automobile and slumped off down the trail alone. She thought that a friendly visit might make him feel, at least for its time, a little less lonely. As an excuse she carried a package of groceries which had been brought out from town for him by Nick Baron.

She tried to keep Nick Baron out of her mind as she followed the trail that Billy had taken. Below the stampmill it led along the bank of the gulch. Above the stampmill the gulch widened out into its watershed but below the mill it was a narrow gorge. Its bed of naked rock strewn with huge boulders was a hundred precipitous feet below the trail. A small stream wound between shallow pools and took to the air over the many falls stepping the gulch down the mountain. A wild country strange to her sight and, for perhaps that reason, somewhat frightening. She was relieved when the trail turned off to the left, taking

her over a fold of the ridge and then dropping her down
to the head of a small ravine that was a tributary of the
gulch.

A rock cabin stood on a level quarter acre bordering
the bank of the wash. Piles of stones up and down the
wash were the milestones of many years of placering with a
rocker. There was no sign of recent work. Under a lean-to
at one end of the cabin there was a hand forge, a goldpan,
some lengths of drill steel, a miscellany of prospecting
equipment. At the other end of the cabin a wisp of smoke
rose from its chimney.

Helen called. There was no reply and she went on to
the open door. Billy Bedrock was not in the cabin. She set
the package of groceries on a scrubbed table and sniffed
the aroma of frijoles simmering with chili on an iron cook
stove. Then she saw the photograph of Saul Baron standing
on a wall shelf. It was inscribed, "To help you remember—
Saul Baron." A brown stain half obliterated the signature.
It was the copy that had been bequeathed to Mr. Parsons.

After the first shock it made sense. Mr. Parsons on
leaving the lodge had followed the trail to tell Billy about
what had happened or Billy had called on him that evening. In either case Billy had seen the photograph and had
been welcome to it.

It took her longer, much longer, to decide what to do
about it. She found a knife and taking the photograph from
the shelf slit apart its bottom edge. With the prongs of a
fork she drew the inserted piece of linen out far enough to
pinch hold of it with her fingers. As she pulled it out she
heard some sound behind her and whirled to find George
Sears blocking the doorway.

His square, pock-marked face was expressionless as he
looked at the photograph in her left hand, the oblong of
linen clutched in her right and, finally, at her. He would

know that she was carrying her own chart on her person. With the one in her hand and his own that would make three. The necessary three.

As his eyes held hers she remembered the prospecting shafts which she had seen along the trail to the cabin, dark and cool with green-scummed water waiting below the uncertain footing of their grass-grown edges. It could be thought that she had stepped too near. It was not surprising if he could read her thoughts.

He said quietly, "You don't need to be nervous, Miss Farr. Sin's been following me with a 30-30. I imagine he's squatting behind a boulder with a bead on my back."

Helen's knees felt weak in relief.

Red Sears stepped within the cabin, removing his hat from his rust-gray hair. He wiped a band of perspiration from his forehead with a folded handkerchief and replaced it in a pocket of his iron-gray suit. His manner was deliberate and unhurried.

"I got to thinking about Billy after I saw you leave," he continued evenly. "I saw there was a chance the photograph might be here. I thought it might save trouble if I could keep you from getting him mixed up in our business." He looked at the photograph. It could be returned to the shelf with the slit in the bottom edge of the mat passing unnoticed. "But I see you've already thought of that," he said.

"Would I be apt to forget," Helen asked bitterly, "after Mr. Parsons?"

She dropped her eyes to the chart in her hand. She stared long at it, her hand shaking, and then raising her eyes, a queer smile on her set face, she held it out to him. He took it from her fingers, held it flat in his large hands. Instead of the long columns of figures only a single sentence was typed upon it. It read:

CHART No. 1

I doubt if this one was worth murder, or even robbery.
He raised his eyes to her bitterly mocking smile.

"What do you think, Mr. Sears?"

His granite face betrayed nothing. After a moment he said quietly, as ever, "I think it was an accident. As a practical matter, Miss Farr, since the charts can't be worked out on a map there's not much gain in getting possession of three of them. A survey takes time and must be done in the open."

She dismissed the explanation instantly without a thought for its practical common sense. She dismissed it simply because her mind was closed to any innocent explanation.

"Then it must be that they can be worked out on a map," she answered impatiently. "An ordinary everyday plain simple map like the one we have," she went on, not giving credence to her own words until she saw in Sears' eyes that she had spoken the fact. If there had been any doubt in her mind before, she was in that moment certain that by following him Sin had saved her life. She returned the photograph to the shelf and stepping to the door called Sin's name.

A covey of crested quail parading in single file on the bank of the wash halted, cocking their heads, and in that instant of their immobility there was the crash of a rifle shot. The quail drummed into the air. A hundred feet from where they had been Sin rose from behind one of the piles of rock bordering the wash. He was wearing his usual dress of a white jacket with khaki trousers, but his black velour hat and unlaced hobnailed boots Helen had not seen before. He was carrying a carbine. He scuffled along the bank to where the quail had been and picked up the fluttering body of a headless bird.

Helen and Sears waited for him in front of the cabin. He came to a stop a full twenty feet from them, apparently not caring to be crowded. The butt of the rifle was behind the crook of his right elbow, his thumb hooked in back of the cocked hammer, his finger on the trigger.

In that position he could fire the carbine from the waist like a pistol. The headless bird hung dripping from his left hand, suggesting that he might even be able to hit something. His walnut-shell of a face was crinkled into the innocent smile of a sportsman who has enjoyed some success in the hunt.

"Like quail?" he said to Helen. His beady eyes watched Red Sears. "Maybe like big game bettah?" he asked. It was not until he added, suggestively, "Gun accident happen too easy," that she realized that his words were much more than a grim jest.

Sears stood silent, careful not to move.

Helen said passionately, "I don't want to hear any more talk of accidents! . . . Please, Sin, there's something I want you to tell me. When Uncle Saul was working in his room—before any one came—do you know what maps he was working with?"

The bridge game at the lodge came to a stop when Helen Farr entered followed by George Sears. Jay Warren Cole rose from his kibitzer's seat when she dropped the chart in the middle of the card table.

"Billy had the photo standing on a shelf," she told them. "We've left it standing there."

Nick was the last one to read the chart. He was the only one not to freeze up after reading it.

He said, "Uncle Saul seems to have had quite a sense of humor."

"Quite," Helen agreed. She was no longer pale. The walk back to the lodge and her burning anger had given her a good color. "To prove how very keen his sense of humor was," she continued, "he left the map that he had worked the charts out on hanging in the office. I asked Sin and that's the answer."

Harry McIntyre suddenly looked ill.

"I thought Price told us . . ." Jeff began.

"Yes," Helen said. "He told us what he knew and added what he believed. Uncle Saul did have all those topographical, or whatever you call them, blueprints, maps or what-nots here, and when he was through with the work he had Sin burn them. That's the point of the joke," she explained sweetly, "because he had not used them. The one he did use he had hung in the office for all to see." She paused, looking at Harry McIntyre. "Whether or not it would have been even possible for him to have used the others is something that I imagine only the mining engineer or," she glanced at George Sears, "the mine superintendent would know."

Jeff was looking at Harry McIntyre. "Not bad," he said. "Not a bit bad. You let us survey up and down the sides of the gulch losing thirty feet in every hundred and then when we're all through and nowhere you take the directions we've given and peacefully work them out on a map of the property and stroll out and pick it up."

He pushed back his chair and rose with clenched fists. Cole stepped between him and McIntyre without seeming to do so. His bland voice was oil upon the rising storm.

"Now I'm quite sure," he assured them confidently, "that none of us mean to make accusations that are nothing but mere surmises! Incapable of the slightest proof! I'm sure none of us want unnecessary complications." He beamed upon them. "Particularly at this time! When, when, my dear friends, we have only to get the map to find the end of our rainbow!"

It took only a few minutes to realize that the map was

not to be found, although they continued to search until dinner time, going through every room in the lodge. It had been left on the dining table when their meeting had broken up at two o'clock the previous morning. No one had seen it since. Sin said he had not seen it when he had set the table for breakfast. His young helper, John, was brought in and denied having seen it. The subject as well as the search was dropped. To talk about it could only make an uneasy situation worse.

At dinner Sin served Helen the quail. To her thanks he responded grumpily that it had been a damn long walk for damn little game. He was in the same questionable temper when she hunted him out late that evening in the kitchen. She found him mixing himself a beverage compounded of white wine, vanilla extract and gin. He blinked slowly two or three times after tasting it and laced another pony of gin into the tumbler; he blinked rapidly and seemed satisfied.

"I want to thank you for looking out for me this afternoon," she said. "With all my heart!"

His wizened face puckered sourly. "You fuss class damn fool," he pronounced.

"But what should I do, Sin? What should I do?"

His answer was quick and definite. He pointed out the kitchen door. "You swipe auto. Go like hell."

She shook her head distractedly. "I can't run away now. I can't be a coward now." She stepped close to him, touched his shoulder with her hand. "Won't you help me?" she asked. "Won't you tell me what to do?"

"Tell?" he shrilled. "All time tell, no time listen, go to hell!" Snatching up his glass, he swung away from her and slammed the door to his quarters.

In the darkness outside the kitchen door Helen saw the glow of a cigarette. "Come on out," Nick said.

"I suppose you overheard?" she asked, joining him.

He nodded. "You sound scared and lonely," he said.

"I am."

"You don't have to be both."

After a moment she replied, "I doubt that."

Nick said, "I don't think you do." She did not try to resist him when he kissed her but neither did she respond. He stopped as soon as he sensed her unresponsiveness; his dark face peering down into hers was, for once, not mocking.

"It wouldn't make me less alone," she said. "Because in too many ways I don't like you, Nick." He released her then and, as on the first night when he had kissed her, she turned and went up the outside stairs.

"Wait." He came up the stairs after her. She caught the cold glint of metal in his hand. "If you've never shot one of these," he said, "all you have to remember is to squeeze the grip when you pull the trigger." He handed her the automatic. "You may return it in the morning."

Saul Baron's funeral was at eleven the next morning; it was mid-afternoon before they were back at the lodge. Billy Bedrock had made the trip with them, Willet Price having brought out his car so that all might attend. The lawyer left at once, not caring for their company, but Billy stayed to dinner. As an excuse for the surveying equipment which they had procured in Sasoon they had given out that they were "interested" in the mine. Billy was delighted with the idea that Dead Finger Fault might be put in operation again. He whiled away the evening for them with tales of lost mines and bonanzas discovered by fortuitous chance or a cryptic message from the dead. . . . His gentle monologues veiled the strain and expectancy with which they waited for the morning and tomorrow's gold.

5

Breakfast was at dawn. Since they had no map, they would have to survey, and the earlier at it the better. When they left the lodge only the Two Saints had picked up the early sun, the ravine being still in the shadow of its eastern ridge. In that high relief of light and shadow the mountain appeared to Helen Farr even more wild and forbidding than usual. Gold? Nothing could have been further from her thoughts. She thought about the scenery, or whether George Sears could use the rod as a pole if he should take into his head to pole-vault; or whether Harry McIntyre found the transit heavy on his shoulder and how clever it had been of Mr. Cole to pick out the light tripod for a plummet. She wondered if she shouldn't offer to relieve Jeff of the axe he was carrying, since he also had a large armful of stakes, and did so. She noticed that Sylvia did not offer to relieve Nick of his hatchet although he was similarly laden with stakes. She thought about everything and anything to keep from thinking about the gold.

But it was, at least at first, easy to take an interest in the details of this survey that was to take them to the end of the rainbow.

Beginning at SE corner monument of Gold Pocket claim . . .

That turned out to be a cone of rock piled around a concrete survey post some two hundred and fifty yards below the lodge between the road and the wash of the gulch. Harry McIntyre set up the transit over the survey post.

. . . the line from same to NE corner monument being the base line 0-360° . . .

Cole hung a plumb line from the tripod over the northeast corner monument. Harry McIntyre set the vertical cross-hair in the transit telescope on the plumb line and the horizontal scale on the transit was set at 0-360°. To Helen's astonishment that was all there was to it; they had actually started the survey.

Any three charts in sequence lowest number to highest . . . They left it to chance. McIntyre ripped a sheet from his notebook and tore it into six pieces which he numbered from 2 to 7. Sylvia drew three of them from a hat. She drew numbers 2, 4, 5: Helen Farr, Jeff Oliphant, Harry McIntyre.

"All right, Miss Farr. What's the Starting Direction of your chart?"

She took it from the pocket of her jacket. Her hands and her voice were unsteady. "'1440 ft. 135°,'" she read.

When the telescope of the transit was swung around to 135° from the base line it pointed in a line diagonally crossing the gulch to the opposite ridge. The discovery that Saul Baron had worked out the charts on a property map meant that the measurements in their survey must follow a level line. Running a measured level line in precipitous country was, Helen soon learned, a task that was simple in principle, tedious in execution, and requiring no little plain hard physical work. In measuring the line the two ends of the tape had to be kept level; it was like measuring the treads but not the risers of an imaginary stairway and marking each step with a stake. The transit had to be endlessly advanced with endless back-sighting for its own alignment; bushes cleared out of the way, trees chopped down . . . 1440 feet to a gully on the eastern ridge.

Then 960 feet of the same business straight up towards the peaks.

1025 feet more over the crest of the ridge and out of sight of Dead Finger Fault. Half through and past noon. No one thought of lunch.

1740 feet diagonally back over the crest and down to the great dump of the tunnel on Sourdough. It was mid-afternoon. It seemed to Helen like mid-afternoon of the next day. She sank down on a wood platform on the edge of the dump and took off her shoes. Jeff squatted beside her. The others were strung out in a line behind. Jeff was attending a bob that hung above a pencil line on the platform. The pencil line marked the end of the 1740-foot measurement. He moved the plumb line a little to the right, back a trifle to the left as Harry McIntyre signaled at the transit. Harry dropped both hands. Jeff let the point of the plummet bob against the pencil line; made a cross mark at the indentation; put the plummet in his pocket and sprawled out comfortably on the platform.

The platform adjoined the head tower of the aerial cableway. The tunnel had been driven through six hundred feet of barren rock before striking the ore body that had been previously located by bore holes from above with a diamond drill. The barren rock had gone to make up the dump. The cars of ore had been emptied into the skip, or aerial ore car, that hung beside the platform from the suspension cable that ran on down the side of the ravine past the shafthead of First Strike to the stampmill on the other side of the gulch. The power cable which, from a drum in the headtower, had held back the loaded skip from plunging like a shell upon the stampmill had, in common with a good deal of the more easily transportable equipment of the mine, long since been trucked away to Sin's profit. The skip was held beside the platform by a trip-bar.

Helen examined what was left of her golf shoes. "If we're going towards the mill," she said, "I'm going to take the elevator. I might as well end in a splash as be worn away by inches."

Jeff did not reply, did not turn his head. He was watching Sylvia and Harry as they came up together. Sylvia had been staying close to Harry all day. Helen did not know what to make of it unless Sylvia had given him her company to avoid the problem of dividing it between Nick and Jeff. She doubted if Jeff saw it in that light. She was retying her shoelaces when Jeff rolled over on his side, facing her, turning his back on them.

"This must be a trying day," he said, "for whoever borrowed the map. A couple of hours more and it'll be about as valuable as a ticket to a show that's over."

The subject of the map had been let drop as too hot to handle. She wondered if jealousy were his only motive in bringing it up.

"I'm surprised that no one's done anything to stop the show," he added.

She sat gazing across the ravine at the lodge, thinking of what Jeff had told her. He had, she believed, told her something that he himself did not know. After a moment she said, "It won't be stopped unless Saul planned it that way."

A hundred yards away was the tilted car beside which they had sat on her first morning at Dead Finger. Jeff remembered how she had that morning sat gazing at the lodge and she had said, "I feel caught in a trap." She had said something just before that. She had said, "I'm scared green." She had not looked green. She had looked just as she did now, flushed with exercise and the sunlight mixed up in her hair. Only her voice had betrayed her fear just as it did now.

"He knew what was going to happen," Helen said. "He knew what was going to happen to Mr. Parsons. He knew what would happen to him if he gave him one of the photographs. That's why he gave him one, so it would happen to him."

Jeff glanced over his shoulder. "Take it easy," he said under his breath, "don't let the strain of this get you."

"No," she agreed. "Oh, no. But it's kinda funny, ain't it, pal, that the only person who knows what's going to happen is a dead one?"

Harry McIntyre, lugging the transit over his shoulder, was hot. He hung his necktie over the conveyor cable, pushed his hat back from a perspiring forehead and quickly went to work setting up the transit over the crossmark on the platform. When it was level and centered he took his backsight for the new base line on a plumb Cole was holding part way up the ridge, checked it with another that Nick was holding farther back. He signaled them to pick up and walked in circles smoking a cigarette.

Cole came down the rise with the nimbleness of a bouncing rubber ball. Sears returned from a stroll he had taken to the mouth of the tunnel. There was some impatience while they waited for Nick Baron. He walked like a man with something on his mind, and when Helen got a good look at his face she felt intuitively that he had thought of the thing which Jeff unwittingly had told her, but that he was of two minds what to do about it.

"Everybody here?" Harry McIntyre inquired with irritation. "All right then. Let's get on with it. My Key Letter this time is G."

Jeff consulted his chart. "1130 feet at 225°."

It took them along the side of the ridge crossing Silver Dollar claim to a point near the location monument on Indian Mine. They began looking around once the last stake was driven and marked. It might be in sight now, where the next and final measurement would lead them.

Jeff said, "The Key Letter is C."

Helen unfolded her chart. Her hands were steady.

2nd HALF
A — 1380 ft. 135°
B — 1090 ft. 270
C —

"1272 feet 270 degrees." Her voice was clear and firm.

The transit was set on the base line that had had its beginning on the platform of the dump of Sourdough; shifted 270° it bisected the shafthead of the inclined shaft on First Strike. That was not to be, however, the terminal of the final measurement The shafthead was, at a glance, much more than 1272 feet away.

The end of the survey was marked by a chalked cross in the center of a bare, unbroken slab of living rock the size of a tennis court.

Nick said, "Only God has buried anything under this."

They combed the ground within the radius of a hundred feet, searched it carefully within a radius of two hundred, drew together again around the blue chalk line on the weathered stone. Nick shook the last cigarette from a package and then, stooping, placed the empty package as a marker for the end of the survey: *Lucky Strike*. It did not amuse any one else.

Harry McIntyre said, "We've been careful about our angles. Slight errors on the tape compensate each other. We could be a few feet off, not more."

Jeff said, "I'd be happy if I had a scale map of these claims. I've heard you and Helen give your directions. I could read mine again—more accurately. Then working on a map with a ruler and a protractor I think I could locate something nice."

So Jeff had thought of it after all.

McIntyre's toothbrush mustache was a dark bristle on his white face.

"You were damned quick to accuse me of taking the map," he said, and his clipped voice snapped like a trap. "Not a bad way to turn suspicion from oneself, is it?"

Jeff took a step towards him and fell to his knees as Red Sears struck him above the temple, a slow, heavy, club-like blow. He shook his head two or three times. He looked up at Sears and raised one knee from the ground, shifting his weight to launch himself to his feet.

Sears said quietly, "We don't want trouble. We can't have the kind of trouble you were about to start with Harry. I didn't come here to hunt trouble. Not with you. Not with any one. I came here to get something else. We all did. We can't get it unless we all work together."

Jeff rose to his feet, facing Sears. "All right," he said. "All right this time."

"I don't want trouble," Sears agreed.

Nothing had happened, absolutely nothing unpleasant, or threatening, and certainly nothing dangerous . . . how the devil Jay Warren Cole managed to put over that idea Helen could not understand, but put it over he did.

He simply said thoughtfully, "I don't think we made the mistake. I think Saul did. He had a great number of combinations to work out. He was a very ill man. Dying! It would be strange if he didn't make a mistake in one of the combinations. We can follow another combination tomorrow. And tomorrow evening we'll have what we expected to have this evening!"

They let it go at that. Helen suddenly realized how tired and hollow she was. She was so tired and hollow that nothing else meant anything. The surveying party slowly returned to the lodge in silence, the Two Saints bright in sunlight above them, the ravine in the shadow of its western ridge. Dinner was at dusk. They went to their rooms immediately afterwards. Sylvia, returning to her room after a visit across the hall to her father, found Nick stretched out on the bed.

She said, "If there's anything I loathe it's shoes and cigarette ashes on a bedspread."

"I can take off my shoes," Nick offered, swinging his feet to the floor.

"Don't shut the door, Nick."

"You could still scream."

"You're clever, Nick, but I'm not going to have Jeff see you come out of my room at night when the door's been closed."

Nick swung his feet back on the bed. She sat down at the dressing table but turned the chair to face him. He looked at her through cigarette smoke.

"I like this," he decided. "Why?"

Sylvia said, "It's so domestic. You're just a home-lover at heart. You'd make a girl a good husband." She smiled at him, her amber eyes unsmiling. "Isn't that the thought you wanted to get over?"

He sat up, rubbing the cigarette out in an ashtray on the bedside table. "I'm more domestic than Harry," he objected. "Or what's the secret of his fascination? That military rank dating from World War One? Probably faked at that."

Her black eyebrows arched. "You're not yourself tonight, Nick, are you?" she asked. "It's not like you to go in for criticism on moral grounds. And not becoming. 'If you can't be convicted it isn't a crime' still suits you and your business better, doesn't it? Or am I to understand that the clients of your financial house never lose anything to the house?"

"We've been operating in Philly for many years—" he began, and then threw it aside. "Why so bitter, Sylvia?" he asked.

She hesitated as if tempted to answer him and then said, instead, "I'm nervous. I'm worried." Her eyes held his. "I'm worried about Jay."

"I don't know," he said. "I don't know that there's anything to worry about. He's only one of six. The odds are in his favor."

"That's not what I mean." She continued to look at him for a moment searchingly, then rose. "I'm awfully tired. You'll have to let me say good-night."

He went down the hall to his room. All the other doors were closed.

Two hours later Helen stepped into the hall and very quietly reclosed her door behind her. It was dark in the hall. She felt her way along the wall, passed Jeff's door to the stairwell, slipped silently down the stairs in her stocking feet. The embers of a log were in the fireplace. She stopped in front of the fireplace to put on her shoes. She was wearing a black coat.

She went in the office. The thin darkness of the starlit night was black indoors. She had to feel her way around. The transit had been stood just inside the doorway to the left with the rod and the small tripod, while the rest of the surveying equipment had been dropped on a desk to the right of the doorway. That was her recollection of the matter but she could not lay her hands on the steel tape. After some thought, she put a ball of heavy cord in her coat pocket and left the office by its outer door.

She went quickly down the road, glancing only once over her shoulder. The windows of the lodge that she could see were dark. When she reached the stampmill she turned off the road. The foot tower of the cableway was attached to the ore bin that rose above one corner of the mill. The cable was a ruled line against the sky. She followed under it to the shafthead of First Strike.

The shafthead was a box-like structure of corrugated iron. Its loading tower, that was connected to the cableway, rose twenty-odd feet from the ground. Helen approached it in the night with the same feeling with which she would have approached a deserted house. Her teeth were clenched tightly together as she stood beside it, orientating herself. When the surveying party had reached the shafthead on their way to the lodge that evening she had, innocently enough, turned and looked back. Now against the stars she again found the outline of a camel's back on the crest of the ridge. She walked towards it, keeping in line with the dip between the two humps. In a few minutes she came upon the bare slab of rock where the last measurement had ended.

At the edge of the slab she found a squat juniper tree. She walked eighteen paces in from the juniper and, on hands and knees, found the empty cigarette package. She replaced it with as heavy a rock as she could carry. The preceding point had been a stake 42 feet away. When she found the stake she tied a knot a foot or so from the end of the cord and wrapped the end around the stake so that the knot was on top of the stake. She tied another knot in the cord at the point where it reached the rock with which she had marked the end of the survey. She put the knot under the rock and stretched the cord back to the stake, where she tied another knot. She gave it a turn around the stake and repeated the process until she had five 42-foot sections, 210 feet of measured cord.

After winding it up in loops in her hand she put the end knot of the cord under the rock and began retracing her way towards the shafthead. The last direction of the survey had been directly in line with the shafthead. They had followed that line for the 772 feet that she had given them as the length of the measurement. On her chart the distance had been given as 1272 feet. She intended to

follow the line the additional 500 feet that she had sub-
tracted at the time of the survey.

Beyond the rock a dip in the ground shut the shafthead
from view. When she came out of it she found that she
was far out of line. The rough terrain spotted with gnarled
junipers made it impossible to sweep the cord over the
ground. She had to return and start over. On the fourth
attempt the shafthead took form against the stars straight
ahead of her. She put a rock on the last knot in the cord
and going back to her starting point took up the end of
the cord. Winding it up, she retraced her steps to the 210-
foot rock and repeated the measurement. The 420-foot
marker found her close to the tower of the shafthead.

With the end in sight her nerve was badly shaken. She
found it more difficult to put out of her mind the inde-
finable sounds which more than once had come to her out
of the silence of the night, or the times she had halted,
breathless, peering into the darkness where she had seemed
to glimpse something that moved. It was impossible to put
it out of her mind that she could have been followed from
the lodge, that at the edge of the circle of uncertain visi-
bility surrounding her there might be some one who was
waiting until she reached the end of her secret survey.

She put the end of the cord under the 420-foot rock
and walked slowly towards the shafthead, paying out the
cord behind her. One knot passed between her fingers,
462 feet. She halted at the second, 504 feet. With an al-
lowance for the inaccuracy inevitable in the rough-and-
ready method of her measurement, she had no doubt but
that the shafthead would have been the end of the 500 feet
on a true survey. She must go inside.

Helen Farr did not like to. She felt less fearful in the
open night. In the open you can run. Very slowly, she
moved to one corner and stood listening and peering into
the night. Memory aided her. She could make out the ore

car on which she had sat for a moment on the morning
when she and Jeff had walked up to Sourdough, and she
knew that just beyond it the tracks dipped into the inclined shaft. Just in front of it there was a switch in the
tracks, one spur running to the dump on the other side
of the shafthead, the other running into the open end of
the shafthead where the ore had been emptied from the
car and carried by a conveyor belt to a bin at the top of
the loading tower for the cableway. There was, she remembered, a narrow passage around the corner between the
rusted machinery and the side wall. It was a planked walk
above the pit where the conveyor belt had picked up the
loads of the ore cars. That would be the first place to look.

As she mustered her courage to turn into the dark interior she was frozen by the sound, distant but piercing, of
a scream in the night. It seemed to come from high up the
side of the ravine towards Sourdough. There was another
sound that jerked back her head, an electric humming over
her head, a humming that seemed to come from the black
thread of the cable stretched between earth and sky. To her
left it stretched away into the darkness down to the stampmill across the gulch, to her right high up to the tunnel
on Sourdough.

Helen remembered the aerial ore car. It was running
wild down the cable. She flattened against the cold corrugated iron of the shafthead behind her as she heard the
scream of terror again. It was nearer, nearer. With a screech
of rusted metal a black meteor tore through the midnight
sky. As it hurtled over her head she saw in a blur against
the stars the head and shoulders of a man. He screamed
as he passed on into the darkness. She heard the scream
end in a drum crash of metal when the skip reached the
stampmill.

Silence had come to the night, a quick, dead silence
and she had seen the stars go out. She had found herself

lying doubled up against the shafthead. She had got to her feet and had unsteadily walked a few steps away from the shafthead. It had been the sight of a distant rectangle of yellow light, lamplight shining through the open door of the lodge, that had recalled her to what had happened.

Now, an hour before dawn, the yellow lamplight from the doorway made a path across the terrace behind her as she stood looking down at the lights that moved through the darkness at the stampmill. There was the globular glow of a lantern and the darting beam of a flashlight. They moved from the stampmill towards the pinpoint of red that was the tail light of the car on the road. A moving figure was seen briefly but sharply as it passed through the white path of the headlights of the car. Presently the beam of the headlights swept farther down the road. Helen turned back to the doorway of the lodge.

Sylvia, too, had been watching. She stepped back from the doorway and preceded Helen to the fireplace where Sin was poking some crackling logs. The wizened old man was Casanova clad in blue-and-white striped rayon pajamas with a white-piped blue-satin collar and a white-piped blue-satin sash with long white tassels. He was wearing them over knee-high hobnailed boots. Sylvia and Helen waited in silence, half-watching Sin at the fire, half-facing the doorway.

George Sears paused at the door to put out the lantern. Jay Warren Cole came on to the fireplace. They both looked like the devil. Helen knew that she must look the same after twenty-two or -three hours without sleep. But, despite sunken eyes and gray cheeks, despite the weariness that dripped from the man, Jay Warren Cole looked himself in his calm self-possession. He placed a flashlight that he was carrying on the mantel and then stood beside Sin holding out his hands to the fire. He was clearly unaware that two women stood rigidly waiting for him to speak.

He sighed heavily and said, as if to himself, "A step too far in the dark."

Then, as if suddenly recalling that there were others present, he turned, facing Helen.

"A step too far!" he repeated. "A single step over the edge of the platform . . ." He shook his head. "If only he'd been more careful when he tried to climb out of the skip! But—reaching for something to grasp—he released the trip-bar. It's the only way it could have happened. The only way."

Again he shook his head, sadly, sadly. "I suppose he was restless tonight, overly tired, as we all were. It's always so hard to get to sleep after a trying day. A stroll to calm the nerves. Very natural. Very. Then no doubt it occurred to him while he was walking that he might as well go on up to Sourdough and get his necktie. Then when he reached for it where he'd hung it over the cable . . ." Cole raised his hands palms upward, dropped them heavily to his sides.

"A terrible accident," he concluded. "Terrible."

There wasn't an opening or a crack or a flaw in it, it was nice and smooth all around like the shell of an egg. Sin's battered touring car was being driven down the mountain by Nick Baron with Jeff Oliphant beside him in the front seat, and on the floor of the back seat wrapped up in protecting sheets was a bundle that was the dead, broken body of Captain Harry McIntyre. But no blow from the world outside was to break into the secret of those remaining at Dead Finger Fault. It would remain nice and smooth all around like the outside of a glass egg. Because Harry McIntyre had not been murdered. His death was an accident, like that of Mr. Parsons. Just another accident.

Helen Farr went up to her room with a cold lump in the middle of her chest. Oddly, she did not feel as nervously apprehensive as she had before it had happened. She felt helpless, like a fish in a barrel, unable to do anything but

wait for whatever was going to happen to her. That numbing sense of helplessness was with her when she propped a
chair under her doorknob, telling her that it was useless,
and it was lying beside her through the long hours until
she went to sleep in the late morning. It arose with her
when she awoke in the late afternoon.

As she left her room to go downstairs she met Jeff in
the hall. Wrapped in a bathrobe, he was just out of a cold
tub. He had ducked his head under the tap and his wet
blond hair had the solid look of the hair of a statue. A
trickle of water followed the blunt angles of his jaw and
trickled from his chin. He looked like a hangover. It was
the first time they had seen each other since the night before. Helen asked if he had had any rest.

Jeff said three or four hours. "Nick and I turned in
after lunch. After Price and deputy sheriff Nordice left,"
he added.

"Oh."

Helen waited for him to go on, relieved that it was
from him that she was to learn what had happened. She
felt more at ease with him than with any of the others,
and much more confident that he would tell her the plain
facts—and all of them.

"It was a sociable call enjoyed by all," Jeff told her.
"Very pleasant chap, Nordice. Understanding. Sympathetic. Price had already explained to him that we're 'interested' in the property and had been doing some surveying. We only had to explain about McIntyre hanging his
necktie over the cable by the platform and," his voice was
edged, "the rest of it. He agreed with us that it was too
bad. He agreed with us that mining's a risky business. You
agree too, of course?"

If he had slapped her across the face with the wet towel
hanging over his arm Helen would have felt about the
same.

She said, tight-lipped, "Why ask? You know how easily my doubts and scruples are satisfied."

Jeff said, "I'm sorry. I didn't mean it that way."

"Of course you did."

"Well then, damn it, I don't mean it now. I know there's nothing you can do about it. It's simply that I don't like you mixed up in this. If I wanted to throw rocks I'd pick on a man."

"Oh, I can see you have hair on your chest."

Jeff wagged his head. "My God, you're hard to make peace with." He watched the temper go down in her eyes.

"I don't mean to be," Helen said. "Not with you. I haven't that many friends here."

"Stranger here myself," Jeff agreed. He seemed to be thinking of something else. "Nordice is going to get in touch with the next of kin," he told her. "He's taken all of Harry's belongings with him. You may as well know that the chart wasn't included."

"No," she said dryly, "I scarcely thought you'd turn that over."

"No, of course not. But we didn't have it to turn over," he said. "It wasn't in his money belt or in his room." Jeff paused, and then spoke as if giving her a lesson to learn. "He must have decided against carrying it with him and hid it somewhere. It's the only possible explanation."

"Yes. Of course." They stood a moment in silence, were on the point of parting when she said, "The steel tape wasn't found?"

"Found?" Jeff repeated. He shook his head. "It was never lost."

"Oh. I thought some one said it was."

Helen went on to the stairs and Jeff to the door of his room. She hoped that her explanation of her question had sounded as smoothly unconcerned as his reply to it. As she went down the stairs it occurred to her that it did not matter; that as soon as Jeff had time to think things over he would realize that he had told her that he had returned the tape to the desk in the office.

There was no one in the lounge. Sylvia and her father were sitting with Nick on the terrace. Helen went into the office. The steel tape was on the desk. She picked up a ball of twine that was on the desk. She remembered where she had dropped it the night before and she remembered that she had not picked it up. She heard footsteps coming down the stairs to the lounge, firm, deliberate steps. Replacing the ball of cord on the desk, she turned back into the lounge.

There were, as usual, bottles of whisky and soda on a tray on the table. A small piece of ice floated in a bowl of water. George Sears dropped the ice in her glass.

"I've so often been where there wasn't any that I don't miss it," he told her. He added in the same even tone, "I untied the knots in the cord."

He had not tried to catch her by surprise because he did not even look at her to see how she took it. He went ahead with pouring the drinks and handed her her glass. Helen set it down again to keep it from slopping.

"All right," she said. "I cheated."

Red Sears lowered his glass from his granite face. "I don't think so," he said. "I think you suspected Harry and simply protected yourself and the rest of us. In case your suspicions were wrong, you went out to find where the survey would have ended. If you'd found what we're looking for I think you would have told us about it. You told us about the charts."

Helen had not made the explanation simply because she had had no idea that he would believe it. He saw her wonderment. He almost smiled.

"I can still recognize honesty in others, Miss Farr."

Her smile was wry. "I'd think you'd remember that my scruples are rather easily satisfied."

"Why, yes," he said. "I think you want the money. The way I see it, you think you're justified in getting it. Saul robbed your father and you think you have a right to get some of that money back; that you shouldn't be cheated out of it because of anything that Saul happened to do later. Raised an orphan, I'd imagine you must feel pretty deeply in debt to whoever did the raising."

Helen was looking at Nick's head outside the window. She said bitterly, "No, I'm just a greedy hypocrite."

George Sears continued dispassionately, "I think you'd be willing to close your eyes to one or two things to get it. But it's something else to be willing to be dishonest in your own eyes. I don't think you want the money that much. I do," he told her. "I think the others do."

"You're being rather honest yourself in warning me not to expect fair play."

"No," he said, "I just don't see where it would be to my advantage if you expected fair play and trusted any one else here."

It was then that she remembered that she had trusted Jeff . . . and Jeff had been out with the steel tape that night.

After dinner they sat around the fireplace until their early bedtime. With the exceptions of Helen and Sylvia, they had little enough sleep in back of them and they were again to get up at dawn and crisscross the gulch with measured lines. Including Helen and Sylvia, they all went to their rooms at once, none having cared to go off and leave the others behind to reach who knows what agreement without him.

Helen was putting on her sleeping pajamas when she saw in the night outside her window the glow of a cigarette. When she could get a dressing gown around her she kicked her feet into mules and jerked open the hall door. As she went down the outside stairs some one came around the corner of the lodge. She knew then, since he was going to face her, that it was Nick even before the glow, of his cigarette as he drew on it gave her a glimpse of a beaked nose, an angular jaw, a flash of eyes under heavy brows. He flipped the cigarette away. They met at the foot of the stairs. He waited for her to speak.

She said, "I didn't think you were a Peeping Tom."

His face hardened. "I was taking a patrol around the lodge," he said. He smiled deliberately. "I wish I'd done so last night," he added.

He could have meant because of Harry McIntyre, but she knew him well enough to know that he was informing her that since she had chosen to take a personal view of the matter he had no apologies to offer. It made her furious that by her somewhat hasty accusation she had put herself in the wrong with him. Her voice was a whip in the dark.

"It's surprising you didn't whistle," she said, fighting it out on that line. "And all this might be very thrilling if I hadn't seen a white man in years. But, as it is, whenever you look at me I feel like I was being pawed by a drunk."

Helen heard him suck in his breath, and then his hands caught her by the shoulders partly lifting her from the ground. Her head was bent back, her face upturned and close to his.

She said to him, "All this can't be passion. Perhaps I'd better tell you I'm not carrying the chart. I've hidden it. So there's nothing to be gained by mauling me."

He let loose of her shoulders as if he wished he were holding her over the edge of a cliff. Helen went back upstairs to her room, quietly closing her door. Presently she heard Nick slam his. She picked up the slip she had taken off. She glanced towards the window and with that glance felt a recurring flash of anger, but knew that it was with herself, and then turning her back on it went ahead and unpinned the chart from where she had fastened it to the slip.

She did not like the idea of going to bed with it. She wished that it were in fact hidden some place as she had told Nick. It would not be needed in the morning, as she was not to be one of the three in the new combination. If all went well it would never be needed again, but if there should be another delay, another night of waiting, she might be far safer not to have it in her possession until it was needed. The only time to hide it was at night

Helen changed her mules for shoes and her dressing gown for her sports coat, turned out the lamp and opened the door. The hall was dark. She slipped down the outside stairs and went down the road nearly as far as the stamp-mill, turning off to the shaft on Gold Pocket. On her first morning at Dead Finger she and Jeff had stood on the collar of the shaft dropping rocks down into the green-scummed water. They then had gone to a three-foot monument of piled stones beside the shaft. It was the location monument of the claim. Jeff had shown her a copy of the location papers kept in a tobacco can stuck down between the stones.

But, once there, Helen realized that a serious draw-back to it as a hiding place was that it might easily occur to Jeff that she had remembered it. She went back to the road and down the road to the stampmill. She had also visited it with Jeff but it was not a place that could easily be searched in an hour or in a day. She did not let herself look up at the square tower of the ore bin that was the end of the cableway. It did not help much simply not to look at it. She felt half ill, shivering at the sound of a stone that rolled from under her foot.

The corrugated metal door in the corner of the mill creaked so that it hurt her teeth. Helen pulled it to behind her and felt in the pocket of her coat for the matches that were there with a package of cigarettes. There were no low windows in the end of the mill facing the lodge. It was the end of the mill the ore came in: to be run from the bin over iron griddle bars for rough sizing and then to the hydraulic breakers that nut-cracked the ore to a size for the battery of stampmills. It was the end of the mill crowded with huge hulks of machinery and heavy scaffolding. With the flare of a match they loomed out of the darkness, dancing in shadows.

Helen stood for a moment gathering her courage as the strangeness wore off and then, holding the match high, she moved towards the soaring pipe organ of the stamp battery. The match burned her fingers and she was again in darkness. As she fumbled in the pocket of her coat for another there was in the blackness ahead of her the clear sharp ring of metal striking metal.

For an instant she stood stock still with a cold shiver running up and down her back and then she turned in panic flight in the direction of the door. It was not more than fifteen feet away but in her first two steps she stumbled over some debris on the floor and fell to her knees. Rising, plunging again into the darkness, she banged against the wall. She felt her way along the wall. She knew that she was whimpering but she could not help it. Her hand touched the doorknob. She flung it open, was outside and was falling, her feet swept from under her, and as she pitched forward there was the numbing shock of a blow on her head.

Helen heard herself moan in protest against the lurching, swaying, head-lolling sense of drunken movement that was her return to consciousness. She seemed to be walking, held up, pushed onward by something that guided her. She knew that there was something wrong, something horribly wrong. She could not get her thoughts straight but her eyes began to clear in the open air.

She tried to step back as she saw the black mouth of the shaft in front of her feet. Something pushed against her shoulders. Before a cry could escape her throat she plunged head first into the void. Twenty feet down she struck the surface of the water with her mouth open as she plunged on down below the surface.

She was half drowned and still sinking in the sightless black before she began to struggle. The sleeves of her sports coat fitted loosely over her pajamas. The coat was unbuttoned. She slipped out of it and regained the surface in time to breathe. Her hands touched things as she treaded water and something soft and slimy bumped against her cheek. She remembered the bloated rats floating in the green scum. The air was suffocating with a decadent stench. High above her head was a square of stars in the darkness. Her hands felt the smooth rock walls.

No cry could be heard over a hundred feet from the top of the shaft. The lodge was nearly a quarter of a mile away. She would not be missed until morning. That was hours and hours away. Many hours more than her strength could last in the cold water imprisoned in the cold stone. All that remained for her was to swim a little while longer in the dark.

6

Jeff was sitting in front of the fireplace when Sylvia came down the stairs. He had not lit a lamp. The fresh wood that he had put on the coals of the fire was just beginning to blaze. Sylvia paused halfway down, and then with a smile came on to the hearth.

"I wondered who it was," she explained.

Jeff said, "I think that whenever I think of this place it will be as being tired and unable to sleep."

Her smile of agreement was resigned. "It was a door about a half hour ago," she said. "I think Nick slammed it. It seemed to be on my side of the hall. I was nearly asleep."

"Yes," Jeff said. "Yes, I heard it, too. Decided I might as well give the place time to quiet down before I turned in. Can I get you a drink?" he asked, starting to rise, sinking back again with his glass when she shook her head. She stood on the hearth swathed sleekly in her Chinese yellow dressing gown, a candle flame in the firelight. Profiled in the firelight, her face had a soft, candleflame beauty.

He said wearily, "I'm a poor liar, of course. What I really had on my mind was you."

Sylvia smiled a little. "You are such a poor liar, Jeff," she agreed. "You're tired but restless and have come to sit by the fire until the lodge quiets down. I was nearly asleep but heard a door slam and that's why I'm up. We didn't waste much time in giving our explanations, did we? Explain why you are where you are and what you've been doing in the meantime. Really I do doubt if we'd think it necessary to do that every time we meet any one if we didn't have one or two things on our minds besides each other. Isn't there enough evasion between us?" she asked gently.

Jeff slowly shook his head. "If you mean about who hit me the other night," he said, "I simply don't know. You keep coming back to it, but I don't know. I don't know why you don't believe me," he persisted, but broke off, seeing her smile.

"Don't you think I know I don't stand alone in your thoughts, Jeff?" she asked. "Not quite alone since Helen came."

Jeff said after a moment, "Let's forget about her. And about Nick, if you can. About the whole damned business."

Sylvia sat beside him.

"And us," she said. "We'll have to forget about us, too." Jeff, scowling, turned his eyes from the fire. "It might be difficult," she admitted. "But we can't think about each other without thinking of them and the whole business, can we? It's so mixed together it's hard to tell where one stops and the other begins."

Jeff sat looking at her. "It's too bad," he said. "It's too damned bad."

A window pane crashed, a banister of the stairway was broken in half, and there was the sound of a rifle shot. The bullet striking the banister jerked their eyes upward to the stairway at the same instant that they heard the crash of glass behind them and then the sharp report of the rifle. Starting to their feet, they stood facing the window before Jeff dropped to his knees in front of the sofa, pulling

Sylvia down with him. They heard some one shout upstairs and then there was the sound of a bullet thudding into the outside of the lodge followed by the report of the rifle.

Jeff said, "That's not close, not close at all."

They heard doors thrown open in the upstairs hall. In a confusion of voices they heard Nick demanding, "Where's it from? Where's everybody?"

They heard Sears reply, "He's outside. Down the gulch."

And then there was a third shot and the crash of the glass of a bedroom window.

Nick called, "Come out of the bedrooms!" He was standing at the head of the stairs.

Farther down the hall Cole's voice was loud with alarm. "Sylvia! Where are you?"

Jeff called, "She's down here with me. Keep off the stairs."

Nick shouted, "Helen! Come out!" They heard him run down the hall. Some one bumped into something in the dining room. John spoke from the doorway. "What's cooking?" he asked, and went on repeating the question in a strong young voice, monotonously if cheerfully seeking a reply.

Nick's voice called from the end of the hall, "She's not in her room."

There was the singing ricochet of a bullet outside the lodge.

Jeff said, "What the hell is this?" He got up and walked around the sofa towards the open door of the terrace. He was halfway there before Sylvia could realize his intention.

"Don't!" she cried, rising. "Don't!"

Jeff shook his head, went on to the doorway. He said, not turning his head. "He's too far away." He stepped quickly through the firelit doorway into the night.

Nick had come running back down the hall to the head of the stairs. "Is she down there?" he called. "Is Helen down there?" He waited a second or two, then started down the stairs, stopping when he was far enough down for his eyes to sweep the room, stopping at the sight of Sylvia standing alone in front of the fireplace staring at the open doorway.

"Jeff's gone outside," she said. "Jeff's gone—"

Her voice was cut short by the report of the rifle.

"Sylvia!" Cole cried out. "Are you all right?"

Nick said over his shoulder, "She's all right. Be quiet!" In the dining room John stopped asking his question. Nick started down the stairs again, slowly, listening.

They heard Jeff shout at some distance from the lodge. Nick ran to the door. There was an automatic in his hand. Sylvia followed him. Cole and Sears started down the stairs. Nick had stopped a few yards outside the door.

He turned and called, "Sin's down the road!" He ran on down the road.

There had been no forewarning. Unchangingly, for a quarter of an hour, there had been the blackness, the dead chill of the water that had soaked the strength from her legs, the aching and then the numbness of her fingers, first of one hand and then the other, clinging wetly to a fingerhold in the rock at one corner of the shaft; and the dark and the cold and the numbness were all that was left of the world to her.

"Helen? . . . Helen?"

Her fingers slipped from the rock. She treaded water frantically, frantically cried, "Yes! Yes, Sin! I'm here! I'm here!"

A falsetto wailing chatter of Chinese had come down to her, only ending in a few intelligible words—"Light! All light! You stay! I call help! You stay! Be light back—"

She had seen the stars again where they had been blotted out by his head and shoulders. A few seconds later she heard, like the snap of some one's fingers, the first of the rifle shots.

Jeff had been the first of the others to call down to her. His voice had been harsh. "Helen! Can you hold out ten minutes more?"

"All right. All right."

"We'll get a rope—something—"

He had left at once, calling out to some one, and then Sears and Sylvia and Cole had joined Sin at the top of the shaft. They called down to her that Jeff and Nick were running back to the lodge to get something to get her out of the shaft. They called encouragingly that it would not be long until she would be out. Not much longer, their voices assured her again and again with the passing minutes. Not much longer . . . not much longer . . . but their words had lost meaning. Her fingers were losing strength to cling to the seam in the rock, her arms had lost strength to paddle, her legs were numb, her shoes pulling down on her feet like lead weights.

Jeff had the better chest for the run up the road, Nick, more lean, the better build. They arrived together, both reeling. Jeff went on the parking space at the far end of the lodge to start the car and bring it to the door. Nick, calling orders to John, went through the lounge and up the stairs straight ahead into his own bedroom. He ripped the sheets from his bed and then raided Jeff's bedroom. Sears' and Sylvia's quickly followed. The motor of the car was coughing in the night as he came down the stairs loaded with sheets and John came in from the kitchen with a flashlight and a lantern. They piled into the car. Nick had tied each pair of sheets together at the corners as he had taken them from the beds. While the headlights of the car rocketed down the road he completed two more knots. When the car jammed to a stop John, cursing

fluently, pushed his face up from the floor where he had
been squatting while he lit the lantern. Jeff grabbed the
lantern and led the run to the shafthead.

Sylvia said, "She doesn't answer us."

Nick said, "Get that damned lantern out of my eyes!"
John turned the flashlight beam into the shaft. A face
floated on the dark water. Water lapped over the face. It
again floated above the water.

Jeff was calling into the shaft: "We've made a rope of
sheets. When we let it down pass it under your arms and
tie it in front."

There was no reply. He straddled the corner of the shaft
above where her head was floating, grabbed the knotted
end of a sheet from Nick, passed it behind him to Sears
who held anchor. Nick dropped a bundle of laundry into
the shaft.

Jeff said, "The knots better hold."

"We'd better see about that," Nick said. He slipped off
his coat and swung his legs over the collar of the shaft.
"You'd better hold, too," he said. "Sin would be annoyed
if there was an accident."

He swung off on the rope, lowering himself hand over
hand.

Helen did not see him. She had seen the end of the
sheet spread out on the water and had released her wooden
hand from the rock to grasp it, instantly sinking. She sank
deeper, her arms powerless, the cold black water pressing
against her open, staring eyes, filling her nose, her mouth.

Looking down as he lowered himself hand over hand,
walking down the wall with his feet, Nick saw the water
wash over her white face, a patch of bubbly scum where
her face had been. He pushed himself away from the wall
and let go.

A cry from Sylvia followed his plunging body. The
stinking water splashed to the top of the shaft. It dripped

from the walls while they watched the churning surface. Jay Warren Cole put a steadying hand on Sylvia's arm as she swayed in leaning over the mouth of the shaft.

The black, lapping water was broken by a splash, a churn of green foam. They saw Nick's dark head. Then he was holding Helen's out of the water by the back of her hair. He caught the rope of sheets above the surface of the water and rested for a moment. Sustaining himself by his grip on the rope he was able to raise Helen higher out of the water, get her arm over his shoulder.

She was conscious enough to try to support herself with her arm, no more. With his free hand he pulled the sopping sheet in and out of the water, passing it under her shoulders, tying it in front, wrapping it around her again and again tying it.

Helen remembered him calling out, "Haul away!"

It was the first thing that she remembered when she awoke at sunrise and found him sitting in the chair at her bedside. The last time she had awakened, but only hazily, dreamily, it had been Sylvia who had been sitting in the chair. And before that at some time in the night it had been Jeff. And before that it had been Sylvia who had wrapped her up in blankets like a cocoon, who had put a hot bag of salt at her feet, who had held cups of hot coffee, syrupy with honey, to her blue lips, and whisky, whisky and more whisky. . . .

Always some one different in the chair at the head of her bed, but unchangingly in the chair in the corner, seen on every fitful awakening, had been the scrooched-up, beady-eyed figure of Sin with the rifle across his knees. She saw now, with the sunrise, that his eyes were red and watery with weariness, and looking into them she smiled into them with a smile of very great meaning. The expression on his wizened face reminded her of a crab apple gone exceedingly sour, and the one change produced by her smile that said, I love you, was a slight increase in the distasteful crinkle of his nose. She knew then that she would love him forever.

She slowly turned her head on the pillow and looked at Nick. It hurt her head when she moved it on the pillow, throbs of pain pulsating from behind her right ear.

"How are you feeling?" he asked, and he seemed intent upon learning.

Helen considered the matter, cautiously stirring in her cocoon, carefully raising her head slightly from the pillow and then letting it sink thankfully back again.

"I creak, but I work."

"This is a bad altitude for pneumonia," Nick said. He pushed a clinical thermometer into her mouth. "Your breathing's sounded all right all night," he went on. "Temperature's stayed a little below normal." When he plucked the thermometer from her mouth he said, "Still there. How's your chest feel?"

She took a deep breath and coughed. She tried it again. There was a band of soreness around her chest where her weight had hung from the rope of sheets. Her lungs felt all right.

"No congestion, doctor."

Nick relaxed. "It's my bedside manner," he explained. He rose. "I'll call Sylvia for you."

Her voice stopped him at the door. "You saved my life, didn't you?"

Nick glanced at Sin.

"Aside from the fact that I'd have been shot if anything had happened to you," he said, and then pausing he gazed musingly out the window opening on the embankment behind the lodge. "Aside from that," he said with a remembering smile, "you're too beautiful to die."

He went on down the hall and Helen heard him knock and call at Sylvia's door. She turned to Sin.

"How did you find me?" she asked in a whisper.

"Look flu mill, look outside." His tone implied that the thing was too obvious to be worth either a question or an answer.

Helen raised herself on her elbows. "It was you I heard! You were in the mill when I came in!"

"How'n hell follow in flont?" he demanded.

He rocked off the chair and shuffled to the side of the bed with bent knees and outthrust head.

"Follow in back, what'n hell all time you chase alound night!" he complained, shaking the muzzle of the rifle under her nose, forcing her head back to the pillow. "One night follow, you get kisses. Two night follow, Hossy-Face fly like boid. Flee night follow, laise hell all clean washee on beds! Godmighty, tly sleep some night!"

Her lips felt stiff. "Who was it, Sin? Whom else did you see?"

"Follow down load," he snapped at her. "Follow off load up shaft. Follow back load. Follow alound mill go inside. Follow—"

"Wait, Sin! Please. . . . You saw me go into the mill—and you went to the opposite end of the mill and entered there—did you make any noise?"

"Why'n hell not?" he demanded defensively. "Bump shinee-bone, cuss hollah like hell! Keep on bump all way flu mill. You hell'n gone. Follow outside. Step on you ciglettes on glound, pick 'em up." He flung on the bed a squashed package of Camels. "Follow alound outside. Follow up load. Know all time you damn clazy, go back off load up shaft." He nodded. "You in."

Helen repeated the gist of it to the assembled company in her room a half hour later. They had dropped in one by one while she was having her breakfast in bed. With the exception of George Sears it was a dressing-gowned group. Without exception she was the first to have breakfast, Sin seemingly not having approved of any one eating until she could. With coffee and eggs inside and some paint and powder on her face again she felt a good deal less like a drowned rat. If after her rescue she had babbled of what had happened, she now could give a concise account of it. She had an attentive audience. Sylvia also had put on some powder and paint, but like the rest of the audience she looked a little gray and drawn in the clear morning light.

Helen said, "I wanted to hide my chart some place. I first went to the location monument beside the shaft." She looked at Jeff. "You showed me the tobacco can with the location papers, you remember."

Jeff nodded. The last one to have awakened, he had had time only to splash some water on his face and give two swipes with a comb to his curly blond hair. His eyes were still puffed with sleep. He had the look of a bad-tempered baby wakened at an untimely hour.

"Then I went to the mill," Helen continued. "It was pitch black inside. I lit a match but it went out. While I was trying to get another I heard a ring of metal in front of me. I turned and ran out. Just as I stepped out of the door some one tripped me and hit me on the back of the head. When I came to I was walking, being half-carried along by some one in back of me with his hands under my arms. My head was just beginning to clear when I was pushed into the shaft. The water washed all the cobwebs out of my mind. I slipped off my coat and swam around until I found a fingerhold. I still can't believe it wasn't at least an hour before Sin found me, but he says it was only fifteen or twenty minutes after he had seen me go inside the mill."

Nick said, "It was around a half hour after I went in my room that the shooting started."

"That would be about right then," said Helen. "I left the lodge about five minutes after you slammed your door."

"Yes," Sylvia said. "I heard it too. It woke me up. It was about a half hour later that I went downstairs."

Jeff said sourly, "I know I decided not to go to bed until the house quieted down. Went downstairs and built up the fire."

Jay Warren Cole smiled wanly. "I think we all must have heard my dear young friend slam his door! I know that I nearly dropped my book I was reading in bed."

"Yes," Sears agreed, "everything had been so quiet I'd thought every one was asleep. Then it was about a half hour when I heard the shots."

Helen Farr found it interesting to learn that none of them had been together at the time she had left the lodge nor until a very few minutes before Sin had stirred them up with rifle bullets.

"When he was following you," Cole said, "Sin didn't see any one else outside?" Helen did not know why the question sounded as if he should have added, "Of course."

"No, he went around to the far end of the mill," she explained. "By the time he entered I was probably outside again. I heard nothing from the far end of the mill while I was inside."

"And he didn't see any one after that?" Cole persisted. It again sounded as if he added "of course" under his breath.

Helen said, "Not until he found me."

"Horrible," Jay Warren Cole said feelingly. He wagged his head. "A truly horrible accident."

His expression was blandly sympathetic as Helen stared at him with widening eyes, and then one after the other she saw that she was looking into wooden faces. She saw that Cole had not spoken on the spur of the moment nor was it just his unsupported idea. She saw that he had discussed it with the others and they had reached an agreement to let her know that what had happened to her had been an accident.

"It's perfectly understandable," Cole was reassuring her kindly, as if she had been caught in some minor weakness. "Perfectly! Please don't think we're accusing you of exaggerating or imagining anything. It's perfectly understandable! Standing in the dark—hearing a noise—*of course* you'd assume there was some one else in the mill!" He beamed at her forgivingly.

Helen said thinly, "Mice, no doubt."

Jay Warren Cole clapped one fat palm against the other.

"Very likely!" he exclaimed. "*Very* likely that's just what it was! But, of course, you wouldn't stop to think of that at the time. I'm sure none of us would!"

Nick said, "We agreed on that last night. None of us would."

Helen said to Jay Warren Cole, "I understand perfectly. I mustn't imagine that some one followed me, and standing outside at the end of the mill threw something—a coin, perhaps—through that big open space just below the roof with the idea that when it struck something inside it would scare me out again. No, no! What I heard, was a metallic mouse. And when I ran out the door I simply tripped and bumped my head. And when I came to again I staggered in a daze on back to the shaft and tumbled in. My dizzy notion that some one was boosting me along and pushed me in was just a girlish aberration caused by the fact that I had it in my muddled head that some one was doing things to me. Now that covers the lesson I'm to learn, doesn't it?"

Cole's bland smile had jelled. "In the calm light of the morning," he said, and a turn of his hand seemed to usher the morning light through the window, "I was confident that you would understand that it was an accident."

Helen nodded. "Just another accident. And just to prove it," she continued sweetly, her temper rising, "I'm going to fish my coat out of the shaft. That piece of linen couldn't work itself out of the pocket."

Sylvia's fingers were curled around the top brass rod on the foot of the bed. Her knuckles were white.

Jeff said, "I'm not trying to do you out of a coat, but we'd better be getting on with the survey."

Jay Warren Cole regretfully patted his shoulder, turned towards the door. "It's impossible," he murmured, "after two sleepless nights."

"Even if we could stagger through the day we could never finish before night," Nick Baron agreed. He turned to Helen. "Will you be able to be up and out with us to-morrow?"

"I'm going to be up this morning," she declared. She flexed her left knee under the bedcovers. "I don't want this to get too stiff to walk. And," she added, "I want to get back my coat." It pleased her to have them on the hip for once. There was only one thing they could say and George Sears said it for them.

"We can give it a try," he agreed, and went downstairs to breakfast. The others went to their bedrooms to dress, Jeff to the bathroom to shave. When he came out he went down the hall and stopped at Nick Baron's door. He put his hand on the doorknob, jerked the door half open and then slammed it. He remained standing in the hall. There was a moment's pause and then Nick opened the door. He looked at Jeff standing there.

"You're cute for your age."

Jeff said, "It's in the interests of science." He came on into the room and again slammed the door. "The control," he explained.

Nick's dark face was getting a little white around the angles.

Jeff said, "That temper again! I do believe you're going to get in a tizzy." He was spoiling for trouble.

Nick said, "I don't know what this is about but I do know I don't like it."

He hit quick and hard with his left fist catching Jeff on the side of the jaw and bouncing his head back against the door. Jeff was rolled along the door by a right that he caught on his left forearm and then he rocked out from the door with a pile-driver right of his own that would have felled an ox. Nick went back fast, two steps, to get away from it, was driven back another step by a pile-driver left that was followed instantly by another right. Nick tried to take another step back and to the left to be in a position to do something about the bull-like charge, but the back of his leg met the edge of the bed as he swayed away from the last blow and it caught him high on the chest. It stretched him out flat on his back on the bed. He jerked up one foot to kick if Jeff took a dive on top of him. Jeff did not want to get kicked in the face. They looked at each other for a moment thinking things over.

There was a light knock on the door.

Nick said, "My God, but some people are polite." He put down his foot and sat up on the bed.

The door swung open and Sylvia came in. She shut the door behind her and stood for a moment with her back against it, her breasts rising and falling under her turquoise sweater with quick, sharp breaths. Her eyes had the look of something that was just about to burst into flame. Her anger was like that, not cold but hot and burning. She looked at Jeff with his fists jammed into the pockets of his bathrobe and she looked at Nick fumbling with a shoelace that was already tied.

She said in a molten voice, "I thought I could trust one of you." She stepped quickly from the door to the bureau and snatched up Nick Baron's automatic lying on top of it. There also was a popular magazine. She hung it over the automatic as she returned to the door. She opened the door, stepped into the hall and slammed the door.

Jeff looked at Nick and said, "That temper again!" He did not take his fists out of the pocket of the bathrobe.

Nick rose. "Not man enough to take it alone," he said understandingly.

Jeff pushed his fists down hard in the pockets. "That's the way it would have worked out if you'd tried to stop her," he admitted. "I think it's much nicer for her to have it. But it was her own idea."

"You weren't signaling her with that slam of the door."

Jeff took his hands out of the pockets. He said, "It was a scientific experiment. I wanted to find out if you can open a door and slam it and still be on the outside of the door. You can. In fact, I think you did."

"So I slammed my door last night just to fool the public?" Nick asked. "Are you trying to make me believe you really think I'd try to kill *her?*" He seemed amused. "You wouldn't know, but she's much too beautiful to die."

Jeff said, "It's too bad we haven't a burlesque show around here we could send you to. Maybe you'd stop peeking. I heard what she had to say to you at the foot of the stairs last night. I think you might readily kill any woman who did what she did to your mannish vanity."

Knowing what he was going to say, Jeff was waiting for a flying fist, but to the face and not the pit of the stomach. It doubled him forward. A swinging left striking him on the side of the jaw knocked him over on the bed. He was not too fuddled or helpless to roll himself across the bed, gaining a few gasping breaths before putting his feet to the floor on the opposite side of the bed.

Nick had stayed where he was. He said, "I was the terror of the seventh grade." Jeff did not say anything. He did not want to waste breath on words. "Yes," Nick said,

"I'm willing to quit now. It's been a pleasure to smack that sanctimonious puss of yours, but I'm here on business, not pleasure."

Jeff did not say anything. He was taking deep breaths now instead of uncertain gasps. He started going around the foot of the bed.

"Think it over," Nick said. He turned and opened the door and went on downstairs to breakfast.

Helen was in no hurry about dressing. Jeff had just got up from the breakfast table when she came downstairs. The others had finished some minutes before and had gone down to the shaft. She saw that Jeff was still in the bad temper in which he had awakened.

"Isn't your jaw swollen?" she asked.

"A toothache," he said shortly.

"Oh."

He continued to look at her for a moment with his eyes a hard blue, and then suddenly he relaxed and gave her a crooked grin.

"I gnawed on some knuckle bones," he explained, "that were tough to chew."

"Things really are progressing, aren't they?" she asked. "First, an accident that might even have been an accident to Mr. Parsons. Then a quite remarkable accident to Captain McIntyre. Then my accident last night—with a little luck I might even have seen my accident. And now . . . blows are beginning to be struck in the open. I'd say we were picking up momentum."

Jeff said, "It was a side issue."

"Name one."

He did not name one. They let it go at that and went down the road to the shaft. The fishing expedition was ready to start work. The cord Helen had used on her midnight survey had been doubled and redoubled into four strands and fastened to a piece of wood to which, in turn, were fastened three large iron hooks from the long unused meat locker at the lodge. The sides of the shaft were only six by four feet and there were twenty-odd feet of air and thirty of water between the top and the bottom. It did not give much angle of pull to drag the hooks. It was a case of drop it, try to wiggle it round a little, and then draw it up somewhat to determine by the pull if anything were hanging from it.

Sylvia, at her own request, was the first to lower the triple hooks into the water. Almost at once she said, "I think I've got something." She pulled in the cord hand over hand. The hooks broke water. She smiled apologetically. "False alarm."

Helen said, "We'll give you one more chance." It was the first thing that any of the rest of them had said since Sylvia had first lowered the hooks into the water.

Sylvia smiled nervously in reply and let the cord slide back through her fingers. It went fast. It slipped out of her hand and spiraled on down to the surface of the water, coiled on the water and sank below the surface. Sylvia licked her fingers that had been burned by the cord. It was a second or two before she seemed to realize that the cord and the hooks, and there were no more, were gone.

Helen thought that it had been very well done.

She smiled at Sylvia and said, "I don't think I'd ever have felt very carefree in that coat again."

Without comment, Nick took a large rock from the dump and dropped it into the shaft. Helen saw that it was good sense. Enough stone on top of the coat would make impossible any private, nocturnal fishing expeditions. The others saw that it was good sense. For some ten minutes they worked hard at dropping large rocks in the shaft, just to see them splash.

No one mentioned the coat or the chart that might or might not be in the pocket of the coat. They were relieved

that they were not going to have to open the pocket. For
the first time in two days there was something like easy,
casual conversation as they strolled back to the road. There
they divided. Cole and Jeff went down towards the stampmill. They gave no particular reason. It seemed to be Jeff's
idea. He probably wanted to put a little distance between
himself and Nick. They were carefully civil to each other,
but they put each other's teeth on edge. Helen and Sylvia
led the way up the road, Nick and Sears following. With
every step they became less chatty. Before they reached the
lodge they were walking in silence. Helen came to a stop.

"I'm going to go down and ask Billy Bedrock back for
lunch," she announced.

Sears made no objection. With a vaguely polite smile
he went on towards the terrace.

Nick said, "It's quite a walk."

"My knee's all right."

Sylvia looked at the lodge and said feelingly, "Let me
go with you. Perhaps he'll ask us to stay at his cabin for
lunch."

Helen said, "I know how you feel."

In fact, she did not know whether Sylvia had asked herself along because she wanted to get away from the lodge
or because she had anticipated that Nick might ask himself along. Nick took it for granted that he was expected to
accompany them and walked back down the road between
them. They saw no sign of Cole or Jeff.

Nick said, "Perhaps they've also tired of our home
atmosphere."

Helen reluctantly admired him. He realized that it was
up to him to make the walk a pleasant holiday and there
was no doubt that he was going to do it by his seemingly
unforced cheerfulness. He was walking between two women
both of whom knew that he had either made love to or had

tried to make love to the other as well as herself and would want to repeat the process with one, of either, or both in the future; and he put them at ease by the simple expedient of letting each of them know by not squeezing her arm or giving her significant glances that he was also not playing that game with the other. It was an admirable performance, but Helen told herself that she wished he were Jeff.

They saw Jeff in the mill. Where the trail to Billy's led beside the mill there were windows of wire-reinforced glass. Sunlight shone into the mill from the opposite side. They saw Jeff standing near the stamps. Cole was standing above Jeff's head on a cross-beam, teetering like a humpty-dumpty as he swung his arm this way and that, evidently describing some operation of the ore processing. His arm swept up and down, his finger pointing from the top of the organlike stamps to their base. Jeff's eyes followed the pointing finger. He was looking down when Cole stepped off the beam above his head.

Outside the window they heard Cole's cry of warning just before he landed on Jeff's back and shoulders, knocking him flat. As the two men sprawled on the floor Cole's right fist swung up and then down like a hammer. He bounded up instantly with something of the horrible agility of a spider. Jeff lay prone and motionless. Cole stepped astride him, bending over him, and again there was that suggestion of a spider in the bloated body and the quickly moving arms and legs.

Helen had not realized that Nick had left the window and ran around to the end of the mill until she heard the door screech open and saw Cole jerk around to face the door. As if awakened from a trance Sylvia turned from the window and, together, they followed Nick to the door. He was standing only a few steps in front of Cole when they entered the doorway.

Jay Warren Cole faced them, legs apart, beaming with triumph. His voice boomed at them in the metal drum of the mill.

"Two!" he cried. "Two! I suspected him—and here's the proof! Out of his own wallet!"

A billfold was grasped in his left hand and from his upraised right dangled two pieces of stiff fabric each the size of a half sheet of typewriting paper.

Helen stared at them with the sickening realization that Jeff had been in possession of two of the charts. She wondered as she stared at them whether the one that was not his own was hers or Harry McIntyre's.

She saw Sylvia slip past Nick and her father and kneel beside Jeff.

7

Sears had gone directly to his room after the fishing expedition for the coat.

In the absence of a key, he propped the back of a chair under the doorknob. He unpacked shirts and handkerchiefs from a bureau drawer, placing them in neat piles on top of the bureau. Then pulling out the drawer he turned it upside down on the bed. Fastened to the underside by gummed strips torn from envelopes was a partially completed boundary map of the twenty-acre mining claims comprising the property of the defunct Dead Finger Fault Gold Mine & Milling Corporation.

Before sitting down to resume work upon the map he leaned out the window to make certain that every one else was still safely away from the lodge. While the chair under the doorknob would protect him against being caught in the act, he preferred not to arouse curiosity by being found barricaded in his room.

The chop of an axe, loud in the silence, had continued to reassure him that John was still cutting a stack of firewood a hundred yards or so from the terrace. A glance in that direction now showed the sunlight still flashing on the swinging blade, while, squatting comfortably in the shade, Sin still supervised, and instructed, and criticized, on the premise that a furious man works furiously. In the opposite direction, down the gulch, Cole and Oliphant were still nowhere in sight, were either still inside the mill or had gone on farther down the gulch. On their way to Billy Bedrock's, the two women and Nick Baron were toy figures beside the mill.

Then suddenly Nick was running back down the side of the mill. He rounded the corner and, jerking open the door, disappeared inside. The two women remained an instant facing a window in the side of the mill and then, running, followed him inside.

With the quickness of not wasting a motion, Sears replaced the drawer in the bureau and the shirts and handkerchiefs in the drawer. He unlocked his suitcase, took out a .38 revolver, broke it for a glance at the loaded cylinder, and tucked it inside the belt of his trousers. He took the chair from under the doorknob and stood it neatly against the wall in the same motion. He ran down the hall to the outside stairs at the far end, judging that there was less chance of Sin catching sight of him than if he ran out the front door of the lodge.

It was characteristic of him that when he reached the last fifty yards of the road he stopped dog-trotting and came up to the mill at an unhurried, watchful walk. He stood in the doorway of the mill within four minutes of the time that he had seen Nick enter it.

His first look inside assured him that neither Cole nor Oliphant had been killed. Jay's face looked like unbaked dough but he was standing on his feet. Jeff was sitting on a low platform in front of the stamps. His shirt and trousers were caked with dust and one side of his head was a smeared mixture of dirt and blood. Sylvia Cole was bending over him, dabbing at his face with a handkerchief.

One glance at the others made it clear that something more had happened than a simple accident. They stood tight-lipped with no word of comment to each other and with no glance of inquiry or sympathy for the injured man. Estimating the situation by his experience of life and people, a broad and often violent experience, George Sears got the idea that something of such importance had occurred that Jeff's injuries would have to be immediately threatening his life for any one to be interested in them, including Jeff. Unless Sears had badly missed his guess Jeff had returned to consciousness just about long enough to know that he was still in one unfractured piece but not quite long enough to know what to do about what had happened to him.

The others were waiting for what would happen. That was the one common denominator between the sickliness that was in Cole's face, the tense watchfulness of Nick, and the stricken look of shock in Helen's widened gray eyes.

Jeff said, "Give me that wallet."

Jay Warren Cole looked at the billfold in his hand as though unwilling to believe that he saw it there. He held it out to Jeff. Jeff sat looking up at him, making no move to take it. The wallet slipped from Cole's unsteady fingers. Jeff did not pick it up. He was looking at Nick, at the two white charts Nick was holding, one in either hand.

Nick saw Sears blocking the doorway, his hand palming the grip of a revolver projecting from his belt.

Nick said, "Jay found two charts in Jeff's wallet."

The others looked at Sears.

"Why, yes," he said without surprise. "I remember him picking it up at the card table." Sears removed his hand from his revolver.

Nick nodded. "That's the size of it," he affirmed. "One's his own, the other, Mr. Parsons'." He looked at it, "'I doubt,'" he quoted, "'that this one is worth murder, or even robbery.'" He handed the charts to Jeff, stood between Jeff and Cole. He said to Cole, "Evidently you don't believe all you read."

Cole said, "When I called you I didn't know." The words were not much louder than a deep breath in the silence. He faced Sears. "I was showing Jeff how the mill operated," he explained. "Out of the corner of my eye I caught sight of the others outside the window. Turned my head towards the window, lost balance, fell on top of him."

He was still speaking very quietly but his voice had become firm and smooth. He was beginning to sound more like Jay Warren Cole.

"Of course," he said, "I gave a shout of warning, but there was not time for him to step aside. My cry attracted the attention of the others outside. As I untangled myself, I saw his wallet lying open on the floor where it had fallen from his pocket. You can imagine how I felt when I saw the folded edges of two of the charts sticking out of it. I believe that any one in my place would have done what I did. I picked them up and called out my discovery to the others, who, of course," he concluded, "had come running into the mill."

Helen felt ill. It was a definite mental nausea. Another of those slick round explanations was being forced down her throat and it was one too many. Sears stepped aside to let her pass out the door. She again went down the side of the mill, but walking fast and with her eyes straight ahead.

Nick caught up with her shortly beyond the mill. He did not say anything. She scarcely glanced at him. Within fifty yards the trail narrowed so that he had to follow in file. Walking fast, her eyes fixed on the trail, Helen began talking. She could keep silent no longer. Too much had been pent up too long.

She said, "He didn't see us at the window. He deliberately jumped on top of Jeff. 'A shout of warning'—yes, when it was too late to warn. A shout of warning to protect himself when Jeff regained consciousness. He made sure he'd lose consciousness! Striking him with his fist when they fell to the floor. He didn't know we'd seen him take the billfold out of Jeff's pocket, didn't know we were there. He was after just one chart—Jeff's. To steal it. Return the wallet to Jeff's pocket. But we barged into the mill right then and so we have a new set of lies, lies, lies, lies!" The word beat time to her sharp, angry steps.

"I'm sick of lies," she flung out. "Smooth, slick lies like hard-boiled eggs, hard-boiled rotten eggs! Mr. Parsons had an accident—a lie. Mr. Parsons was murdered. Some one went from the lodge to his cabin that night. Went there to get his copy of the chart out of the photograph. Mr. Parsons woke up and was murdered. Then the dynamite 'accident' was arranged as Captain McIntyre said it could have been arranged. An arranged accident just like his own turned out to be!"

She did not turn her head to see what the effect of her words might be upon Nick. She was not giving a thought to Nick or the effect of her words.

"It's a lie," she said, "that Captain McIntyre tramped up the mountain in the middle of the night to get his necktie. He went up there because that was the point on the survey where he'd given us a false measurement or direction. He went up there to start a true survey from that point. It's a lie that he slipped and fell into the skip when he reached for his necktie hanging over the cable. He was followed or met some one or went with some one who knocked him out; and took his chart and then dumped him into the skip. It's a lie that he tripped the catch by accident in trying to climb out of the skip. He wouldn't have been dumped into it if the person who was his accident hadn't meant murder—just as that person meant murder when he dumped me into the shaft. All these accidents are lies and we know that they're lies!"

She was out of breath and words. Her steps slowed to a more normal rate of walking.

Behind her, Nick said, "Feel better now?"

"Yes, I feel better"; her tone was not friendly.

Neither was his: "You're a fool."

Helen turned on her heel so sharply that he nearly ran into her. He did not wait for her to demand an explanation.

He said, telling her, "If you're not willing to keep your mouth shut you're a fool for letting any one suspect that you won't."

"All right," Helen said. "I'm glad I talked too much. I'm glad it's brought something into the open. I never imagined that there was any one here who thought I'd keep my mouth shut about murder."

Nick was smoking a cigarette. The smoke curled out from his nostrils as he stood looking down at her. It was a look she had not seen before. It was completely impersonal.

He said, "If you have the slightest factual evidence of murder I suggest you take it to the authorities."

"Evidence?" Helen repeated bitterly. "You know there's none."

"That's why you've been willing to keep your mouth shut?"

"Because it wouldn't do any good to open it? Yes!"

He left the cigarette in his lips. "Accidents are likely to happen in a mining country," he said. "There may be another one."

Helen took time out. It was supposed to be what she wanted. She wanted things in the open, didn't she? Where you can stand up and face 'em. Stand up on weak knees and face 'em.

"All right," she said. Her voice sounded better than she felt. "All right," she repeated. "We'll say there may be another one." She wished that he would change his expression, that is, get one.

"We'll say that there's no evidence," Nick said. "No factual, concrete evidence that it isn't an accident. What do you do?"

Helen said, "If I thought there was going to be another one I'd leave here now. Right now."

"That's all right," he told her. "That's a good idea."

Helen nodded. "I thought that was the idea of this. To try to scare me into leaving."

Nick Baron said, "Don't be too sure about leaving. Not if every one here gets the idea that you're going back on your bargain and double-cross us. You said your scruples were satisfied. Your bargain was to keep your mouth shut about this inheritance we're after."

Her anger was gone; all gone. There was nothing left but the feeling which, if she lived to leave, she would forever associate with Dead Finger Fault. Loneliness was a part of it. The loneliness of the sky, of the distant shimmer that was the desert, of the mountain . . . the loneliness of being in a strange house with strangers, of walking alone in the night, of standing alone on a narrow trail above a deep gorge arguing a matter of life and death with a hawk-nosed man. Fear was a part of it. Fear of the man facing her on the trail, fear of the others, fear for herself and fear for the others. And something else was the rest of it, something that gave her a deep and a bitter anger for the person of Nick Baron.

She said, "If there's murder, this inheritance is the motive. If there's murder, I won't keep quiet about it."

"If," said Nick.

Yes, it might be another accident. He was repeating that question, making her face it. Helen met it head on.

"There's no if about it," she said. "If there's another accident, it's murder, and I will tell the whole wide world that it's murder."

It seemed a long time that Nick stood silent, looking at her. Then he turned aside and flipping his cigarette watched it fall to the bed of the gulch far below.

He said casually, "It was about down there that Billy found Sam's body." He was smiling. "Or haven't you heard the story?"

"No," said Helen. "I haven't heard the story."

"You'd better," he said, "or Billy'll take the rest of the day in telling it."

She had almost forgotten that they were on their way there. She started down the trail again.

"There are really two stories," his voice kept pace behind her. "The historical record is that some twenty years ago, twenty-six or -seven I guess, Billy was prospecting up here with a prospector named Sam. When Billy came back from town with a burro load of grub one time he found that Sam had been killed by a fall down the gulch along here. Then, about a year later, Billy came back on another prospecting trip and staked the claim that he sold a short while after to Saul. We now," he announced, "take a step from history into historical romance."

He was telling the story with zest. Perhaps he simply found it amusing. Perhaps she was wrong in feeling that he had some other purpose in telling it. Perhaps, incidentally, she was a prize ninny to feel so much more comfortable now that the trail had turned off from the edge of the gulch. She took a deep breath of air. It was wonderful air when you could breathe freely enough to enjoy it.

"And then," Nick was saying, "after buying it, Saul began writing up the prospectus to sell stock. To begin with he changed plain Sam's name to Sourdough Sam, and that was a touch of genius. Sourdough Sam, the Klondike, bags of gold dust on the bars in the movies, rags to riches!"

The trail had widened enough for Nick to walk at her side. Helen found herself smiling in response to the compelling good humor in his voice, in his eyes, in the amused curl of his lower lip.

"The next improvement," he said, "was to have Billy remember that when he'd found Sam's body that Sourdough had had a piece of ore clutched in his hand. A piece of rich ore clutched in his left hand," Nick amplified, "and his right arm stretched straight out with the index finger pointing at a fault in the formation in the side of the gulch. 'And that, dear friends,' I'm quoting from the prospectus," he explained. "'And that, dear friends, is the story of a crusty old prospector's devotion to his pard . . . and the discovery of the great bonanza that, *in memoriam*, has been named Dead Finger Fault.'"

It suddenly wasn't funny any more. Helen came to a stop.

"Are you trying to tell me that Billy was one of the swindlers?" she asked slowly.

Nick smiled. "Don't hold this story against him."

"I don't," she snapped. "Didn't he spend a whole evening telling us about gold strikes? And how were all of them found?—A discouraged prospector's down to his last pot of coffee and he happens to upset it and the coffee washes some dirt off a rock—and there you are! It's a nugget. Or a prospector meets another old desert rat who's dying of thirst, his tongue too swollen to talk, but he scratches a map in the sand. Or a prospector's so discouraged he throws his prospecting pick away and it knocks a piece of rock off the side of a canyon and it rolls down to him and there you are!—gold. For heaven's sake," she said, in a temper, "don't you know those tales are meat, drink and tradition to him? That's the way mines are supposed to be found! What sort of a story would you expect him to tell about finding his own mine? What's more," Helen concluded, "I believe it!"

Nick's dark face was flushed. He turned away from her and sat down on a convenient boulder. He laughed so heartily that tears ran down his cheeks. Helen's temper went down but she did not join in his amusement. She did not even feel a little silly, her interest was so completely focused upon Nick Baron.

She would have understood any one being amused at the fine, free, uncalled-for vehemence with which she had gone off the deep end. Perhaps not many would have found it funny enough to laugh so loud or so long, but there was no doubting the sincerity of his amusement. For the matter of that, she reflected, there never was. Sardonic sneer or good-natured laugh, there was never anything forced about it. Nor, regardless of the circumstances, though tempers and violence might be hanging by a hair, did he ever try to restrain his peculiar sense of humor.

Helen straightened the edge of her white Angora sweater, curled up in walking, and raised her arms to tuck in a loose curl of her windblown hair. She saw that Nick had stopped laughing enough to look at her with a new interest. Clearly, he approved of her figure as revealed by her pose and the sweater.

The way she was studying him turned his attention from even her figure.

"A penny for my thoughts," he offered.

Helen was still tired of evasions.

"All right," she said. "You're thinking you'd like to make love to me. Just before this last thought you were captivated by my personality. You were thinking it was not only very funny but also very attractive the way I go all out for dear old Siwash when I lose my temper. Just before that, from the time you changed the subject back at the gulch, you were amused at seeing me amused at a story that you knew you were going to give an ending to that I wouldn't like."

Nick had stopped smiling. He got up from the boulder.
"Double or nothing," he said.

"That's fair enough," Helen agreed. "I'm thinking of
Jay Warren Cole," she said. "I'm thinking how friendly
he is. So that every time he pats my shoulder I feel in
need of a shower to wash off the soft soap. But you're not
like that," she stated flatly. "You get a response from me.
You're a very magnetic person, you are."

He knew that there was a catch in it; he waited for it.

"I'm just beginning to understand why," Helen said.
"It's because you're perfectly frank and sincere in how you
feel about people. That's how you get away with murder.
Because how you feel about any one, one way or the other,
has no effect upon your plans, nor will you let any one
stand in your way."

For a second time after a long thoughtful silence Nick
changed the subject.

"We were talking about Billy," he said.

Helen made no reply. They started walking again.

"I think what riled you," he continued, "was the idea of
Billy having been used as a stooge by Saul and Company.
He possibly did help influence some of the suckers who
were brought out here because he honestly believed in the
mine. Saul and Company did enough diamond drilling to
know that there was nothing but a few rich stringers and
small pockets of gold ore. Nothing to justify a great sale
of stock because the value of the ore wouldn't equal the
cost of mining it."

Helen did not like these abrupt changes of subject. She
had begun to get the idea he had twice chased her out on
the end of a limb and left her there. She listened to him
less interested, at first, in what he was saying than the way
in which he was saying it. She had become accustomed to
almost anything from him except a simple, sympathetic
discussion of a subject or person.

"But Billy believed that it was a bonanza," he said. "He's not a cost accountant. All he knew was that three men and a boy could scratch out the surface stuff, pack it down to the railroad on burros, and end up several thousand dollars to the good. He'd never found anything like that before, naturally to him it was a bonanza. He still believes in the mine," Nick continued. "He believes it's 'where the gold comes from.' The placer gold you can find in nearly every wash around here. Yes, you can find it," he assured her. "But not in large enough quantities for a man to make beans placering. Except Billy's present claim. I understand he takes out between three and four hundred dollars a year. That keeps him in beans, flour, bacon and coffee, and what more could he want?"

Helen found that she was listening with congenial interest and caught herself up short. He's making a sale, she told herself. He's gaining your confidence so that he can put something over. Just wait and see.

"Billy had been prospecting since he was a boy," Nick was saying. "And he must have been past forty when he staked his claim on Dead Finger. Then Saul comes along and makes his dream of discovering a bonanza come true. It's not surprising that Billy was devoted to him."

"Yes," Helen agreed. "I've thought of that. I wonder if Saul didn't like him too?" Her tone was wry. "Since he didn't leave him one of the bequests. . . . But it's a pity Saul didn't leave him something," she added. "It's pitiful Billy has to cherish the photo that Mr. Parsons spat upon."

Nick said, "Yes, it must have been a blow. Naturally he must look upon the rest of us as intruders. He may be as jealous as a woman scorned."

They had gone on a half dozen steps before Helen's thoughts had followed his idea far enough to see where it led. For the third time since he had joined her on the trail she stopped short, facing him.

"So this is what you've been leading up to all the time," she said. "Generously proving that Billy wasn't a swindler—so that you can imply that he may be a murderer."

Nick was unmoved.

"Take it easy," he said. "You're the only person who's even implying that anything's happened except a couple of unfortunate accidents. But if you want to call them murder you must remember that there must be a murderer. It's unfortunate," he concluded, "that some people might question that Mr. Parsons gave Billy the photograph. There's nothing connecting any one else with either accident."

He gave her plenty of time to see how simple it was: *Keep your mouth shut about murder, now and in the future, unless you want Billy Bedrock picked as the murderer.* Just as simple as that.

"If you don't mind," she said at last, "I think I'd rather finish this walk alone."

Nick said, "I do mind. I want to see for myself that Billy still cherishes my dear departed uncle's sweetly smiling face."

Propped against a coffee can on a shelf in the cabin, Saul Baron's face, behind the brown stain left by Mr. Parsons' tobacco juice, smiled down upon Billy, seated at the table, and Billy smiled back. Billy continued to smile when his gaze lowered to the pill bottle of small gold nuggets that he held in his hand.

He had found *that* little rascal after a gully-washer rain, be three months ago now, 'way down in the lower foothills; mighty promising place to do some more prospecting, mighty promising. And *that* little beauty, darned if it hadn't winked up at him as pretty as a brown-eyed girl in a blue hat, winked right up at him, it had, from that bed of basalt in the gulch; yes, sir, wasn't a man the whole country around, and they all did a little prospecting now and then, wasn't a man of them wasn't jealous the eye he had for the little beauties and how they winked up right back at him.

It would hurt him right bad to have to send them off to the assay office, like as bad as for a youngster to part with a bevy of sweethearts. He cocked an eye at the coffee can standing beside Saul's picture. Twenty-eight dollars greenbacks, sixty cents silver there was in it, but he would need that to live on next couple of months. Anyways it wasn't enough to buy a hundred-dollar tombstone. That's what the graveyard man said it would cost, the one with the angel, complete with the writing cut right into the concrete:

Mr. Parsons, Died By Dynamite, and the date.

Billy looked up at Saul and smiled and was glad that Saul smiled back. He rose and set the pill bottle in front of the photograph, knowing that Saul liked nuggets too, never knew a man to like them more. Then from a box under his cot he took out an iron frying pan that he did not use in cooking and a heavy jug. He put the frying pan on the table and from the jug poured out a considerable quantity of quicksilver. Near the stove was a barrel used as a flour bin. He rolled up his sleeve and thrust his arm down into the flour.

After dusting the flour from his arm and rolling down his sleeve, Billy again sat down at the table. One after the other, he submerged three twenty-dollar gold coins in the mercury. He then went to work on them with the blade of a knife, scraping off the amalgam as it formed, hastening the dissolution of the gold into the quicksilver. When the job was done he sopped a small canvas bag in water, thoroughly wetting it, and then poured the soupy amalgam into the bag. Twisting the neck of the bag, wringing it, he squeezed out a considerable amount of bright quicksilver into the pan. He poured the extracted mercury back into the jug.

Opening the bag, he took out a doughy lump of amalgam of a pale gold complexion. He put it in a saucer. As he gathered up his equipment he saw his visitors approaching on the trail a hundred yards or so from the open doorway. Billy smiled happily as he put jug, pan and bag back in the box, as he set the lump of amalgam in its saucer like a votive offering beside the pill bottle in front of Saul Baron's smiling likeness, and he smiled more happily than ever as he went from the cabin to meet his guests.

It had, Helen thought, been something like love at first sight between her and Billy Bedrock. Heaven knew, considering her company at the lodge, it was not surprising that she should take this gentle silvery ghost of a romantic West to her heart, though why he had done the same to her, only heaven knew. But the fact was very pleasant as he showed her over his claim with the pride of a suburbanite showing his garden. It was a relief not to have to talk to Nick, to be able to ignore his very presence.

Billy said that he used the Cloudburst System of placer mining. Come a cloudburst, the gold-bearing soil was washed down the sides of his ravine and boiled over the series of catch basins he had blasted in the bed of the ravine. Gold, being heavier than anything else, sank to the bottom of the catch basins. Pass the cloudburst, each catch basin was a pond, providing both the water and the concentrated auriferous dirt to scoop out into his long tom.

This latter was a box and an inclined trough that could be rocked from side to side. The box was the highest part of the contraption and had a perforated sheet-iron bottom. Pay dirt and water poured in the box were washed and rocked on down the trough. On the bottom of the trough, or sluice, were numerous transverse bars of wood called riffles.

Helen liked this mine. It was simple enough to understand.

"I know," she said. "The gold settles behind the riffles and the sand washes on away over their tops."

"Make you a partner," Billy offered.

"Depends," Helen temporized. "Do I scoop the mud into it or scoop the gold out of it?"

"'Malgam," Billy corrected her. "Last few years been putting quicksilver back of the riffles," he explained. "It catches all the gold no matter how fine, even flour gold and that's the very finest of all."

His innocently smiling eyes were like a baby's, Helen thought.

"For certain's made a difference," he said. "Never had any idea how much gold I used to miss before I caught on to the 'Malgam Method. Don't have to work half as hard to get twice as much. Like to see some 'Malgam?" he asked with the artless eagerness of a gardener wanting to show a prize bloom.

"Lead on, Pard!" Helen said.

He led the way to the cabin. Helen was glad that even Nick expressed wonderment at the size of the lump of amalgam. Billy's innocent pleasure was a joy to behold, but not Saul Baron's smile. Not the fact that his photograph was in Billy's cabin. Helen tried to put it out of her mind when they sat down on a bench outside the door. She did not have any luck. Vacation was over. She thought of other things while Billy told about the amalgam.

It was, he related with childlike pride, the clean-up from the last shower. Of course it wasn't all gold, he admitted, not by any matter of means. But distill off the mercury, and he'd guess there was just about exactly three ounces of gold—a hundred dollars at the new price of gold, after assay charges.

"From one shower?" Nick said. "My God!"

"Oh, there's gold in these hills," Billy assured him. Helen found his dreamer's eyes turned upon her and she tried to present a bright face of interest. "You just have to know where to look for it," he explained complacently. "That's the trouble up to Dead Finger, nobody's ever looked the right place."

"A hundred dollars from one shower," Nick repeated. "My God."

"They just didn't look in the right place," Billy persisted. "The tunnel on Sourdough should have been on this side the gulch," he continued, and continued and continued to expand upon his theory. He took a stick and scratched a map on the ground. He sketched in the locations of the claims. Not that he could fit them together just exactly right, he admitted. "Have to look up the location papers in the monuments to do that."

Helen found that Nick was looking at her over Billy's bent head. She also found that she was getting gooseflesh. She got up and stood in the sun. She tried to make her voice very casual.

"But with the location papers," she said, "with them you could make a perfect map?"

Billy seemed surprised. "Why, yes," he said. "Fact, don't know how else you could."

Nick Baron also rose.

"Sorry I have to be getting back to the lodge," he said.

Billy looked hopefully at Helen.

"I'm sorry," she said, "but I must, too."

They did not need to discuss the matter on their walk back. They went straight to the shaft by the mill. The rocks of the location monument had not been included in those dropped on top of her coat. Nick took the tobacco can from the monument and, as Helen had expected, it was empty.

They went to three more location monuments. In each case the cans were present, the papers gone.

Nick said, "I don't think we have to go any farther to get the idea. I wish I had got it first."

"So it wasn't you," Helen said dryly.

They did not say anything more as they went back to the road and up to the lodge. George Sears was sitting alone on the terrace. He had been watching them. When they came up to him he said:

"The papers must have been taken the night we received our legacies. I looked for them the next day."

Nick nodded. "Any one who'd been connected with mining would think of that," he said.

"Like myself," Helen said acidly, annoyed at the adroitness with which he was putting himself beyond the scope of suspicion. "Jeff and I looked at a set of them the day after I got here. If I'd had wit enough to remember the meaning of what I'd read, I'd have known that a map could be made from them myself."

Sears said quietly, "The important thing seems to be that we may assume that some one *has* made a map from them. He must intend to use it."

Nick glanced at the sun. "Then he hasn't many hours to get ahead of the pack," he said. "We survey in the morning."

Sears said, "We surveyed yesterday."

Helen met his eyes. "Yes," she said, "we could go on surveying like that forever, couldn't we?" She turned to Nick. "The last measurement I gave, yesterday," she explained, hating it, "was a false one."

Nick looked at her a long time. "Without a scruple?" he asked.

"My story is," Helen went on, thin-lipped, "that I did it because I had a strong hunch that Captain McIntyre was trying the same trick. I now think that Jeff had the same hunch because he took the steel tape out of the office that night. Yes, rotten of us, wasn't it? But, of course, tomorrow Mr. Sears and Mr. Cole will trust you, and you just as implicitly will trust them."

Nick and Sears looked at each other thoughtfully.

"Finish," said Nick.

Sears slightly inclined his head. "We've got to play a new game," he affirmed. He rose, his open coat revealing that his revolver was still tucked inside his belt. "I hope," he said, "that no one causes trouble."

8

Helen felt like a tightly wound spring, as she preceded Nick Baron and George Sears into the lodge. Jeff looked up from a drink that he was pouring. The side of his face that had struck the rockdust on the floor of the stampmill was swollen and inflamed. A strip of tape over a gauze dressing covered the cut on his forehead and he had dabbed iodine on the sandpapered flesh over his cheekbone. Cleaned and patched up, his hair combed and in a change of clothes, he looked a lot better than he had in the mill but there did not appear to have been any change in his state of mind. His state of mind appeared to be that of a man who has been slugged in the dark and is looking for some one whom he can hit back.

Nick said, "Where's Jay?"

Jeff did not answer. He was looking at Helen as she stood with her hands holding tight to the back of a chair.

"You look like you could use a drink," he said.

Helen shook her head. She was afraid that a drink would let her down and she would not be able to pick herself up. She saw Sears go to the door of the office. There was the click of a typewriter behind the door. Sears had probably been hearing it as he sat on the terrace. He opened the door and said, "Come in, Jay." Helen saw Jeff's face harden.

"Where's Sylvia?" she asked quickly. It only had been Sylvia beside him in the mill that had kept him from violence.

Jeff looked troubled. "In her room," he said.

He took a deep drink. When he had come from the stampmill he had gone directly to his room to doctor his face, slamming the door. The slamming of the door was what stuck in his mind because he was, now, not sure but that Sylvia had been close behind him. It had taken him about a half hour to get his face fixed up and then, after changing his clothes, he had gone down the hall to her room. Behind the door, not opening it to his knock, she had said, "Please, Jeff, not now." He had gone back to his room and stretched out on the bed for a while, leaving the door open so that he could hear when she left her room. Finally, he had come downstairs to wait for her. As he had come down the stairs Cole had quickly left the lounge for the office and had closed the door. He had continued to wait for Sylvia but had not gone to her room again because the more he thought of it the less he knew what to say to her. He had seen in the mill that she knew what her father had really done.

Sears turned from the office door. "We don't need to have her in on this," he said.

Helen released her grip on the back of the chair and went to the stairs. She said, not turning her head, "I want her in on it." She went on up the stairs. Behind her she heard Sears say:

"A little conference, Jay."

Cole's voice was doubtful. "I've some very important business letters to get off," he said. "I want to make the westbound afternoon train."

As she went down the hall Helen wished that she had never got off that westbound afternoon train. She knocked on Sylvia's door.

"There's a meeting downstairs," she explained. "I wish you'd come."

Sylvia seemed undecided. She did not look her usual self. Her dark beauty was unchanged, but it was less vivid. That was it, she seemed much less alive than usual, more remote, drawn far within herself.

"I think you'd better," Helen urged.

"Yes," Sylvia said, "I can't avoid facing him forever, can I?" She sat down at her dressing table.

Helen remembered how Sylvia had looked up at her father while bending over Jeff in the mill. She remembered how Jay Warren Cole had met that look. She suddenly realized that it had not been fear of what any of the rest of them might either say or do that had made Cole look deadly ill, but it was that Sylvia had seen what he had done. Helen became aware that Sylvia was studying her in the mirror of the dressing table.

"We saw what we saw, didn't we?" she said, turning from the mirror. "So there's not much sense in trying to pretend, is there?"

Helen said, "I've been a blind fool. I haven't known what all this has been meaning to you."

Sylvia asked quietly, "You mean to learn that my father was a swindler? To have Nick carefully explain how big a swindler he was, to make it quite clear in front of you, Jeff, every one? It made it easier," she said. "It helped a lot that you seemed to take for granted that I had always known." She rose from the dressing table. "It was easier than having you ashamed for my sake. Believe me, it's much less embarrassing to be thought a partner in crime."

She picked up her handbag from the table and went to the head of the bed. She smiled a little as she put her hand under the pillow.

"But perhaps you were right the first time, Helen. I may be just a gun moll at heart." She drew an automatic from under the pillow, put it in her handbag. "Nick's," she explained.

No one was talking when they came down the stairs. Nick was at the table pouring a drink. Sylvia joined him. Nick gave her his Scotch and poured himself another one. He gave a nod to Sears.

Sears said, "We've been planning to survey tomorrow. We'd better plan to make it more successful than the last time."

Cole was standing at the fireplace looking at the cold hearth. He said, not looking up, "I'm confident that it will be. We were simply unfortunate in striking a combination in which there was some error in Saul's calculations."

Helen knew that that was her cue. She saw Sears and Nick looking at her, waiting. She looked at Sylvia as she answered.

"Another reason may be," she said, "that I gave a false measurement." She saw the startled surprise in Sylvia's almond eyes, and then as it had time to sink in she saw a flash of mirth. Helen looked at Jeff and saw that he was not surprised.

He gave a nod in answer. "I think you know I had the tape out that night. Yes, me too," he said. "Look sanctimonious somebody," he invited. He was looking at Cole.

Jay Warren Cole returned the look. He said, matter-of-factly, "I'd have done the same in your place. Without speaking ill of the dead, I may say that I would have feared that Harry would play the same trick."

Nick said into his glass, "Without speaking ill of the dead, may I suggest that it's Saul who's played the trick?" He raised the glass to his lips.

"No," Sears argued. "There's no doubt Saul had the gold. His safety-deposit boxes were opened, were empty. There's no doubt he hid it here."

Nick lowered his glass.

"Yes," he said. "Oh, yes. It's here all right. And we have, I believe, true directions telling us where to find it. Only we have to work and share together to make any use of 'em. Only I don't trust you and you don't trust me and we're both sure that either Jay or Jeff would double-cross either of us. Helen, of course, has scruples. But since she doesn't trust any of us she has to double-cross us all in self-defense. Let me repeat, Saul had a sense of humor."

Sylvia said, "I think the Greeks had a couple of words for it." Her smile was bitter.

"Poetic justice?" said Nick. His tongue licked out on the sardonic curl of his lower lip as if picking up a tasty morsel. He washed it down with a sip of Scotch and soda. "Why, yes, it may be," he agreed easily, "that we're only suffering the sins of our own evil natures."

Sears said, "I don't give a damn."

When he said it Helen realized that she had never before heard him use any word of profanity. It was a danger signal. He took a step or two forward, placing himself in the center of the group.

"The only thing I give a damn about is finding the gold," he stated. "Without any more delay. Without any more trickery."

Looking at Cole, Jeff said, "That sounds fine."

Cole kept looking at Sears. "Yes, Red," he said earnestly. "No more delay, no more trickery."

"Hallelujah!" said Nick. "We've got religion. Now we can trust one another."

Cole said, "That will not be necessary. Not if we sit down and openly inspect one another's charts and work out together the course of the next survey."

Nick set his glass down on the table.

"Since you're willing to stop trying to be a lone wolf, I am," he consented. He took a billfold from his inside coat pocket. "Now?" he asked.

Sears nodded. "Right now."

Jeff said, "I'm damned if I will."

Sears had reached for his hip pocket. He slowly turned to face Jeff, his hand still at his hip, and then slowly his hand moved nearer the grip of the revolver under his belt.

"I don't want trouble," he said quietly. The words were more than quiet, they had a deadly calm. "But delay means trouble. If we're going to have trouble it might as well be now."

Helen was standing so that she looked past Sears towards the table. No one else was looking that way. She saw Sylvia open her handbag and put her hand inside the bag and then the bag was pointing at the middle of Sears' back.

"All right," Jeff said, "let's have this trouble."

Sears said, "Get your chart."

"Go to hell."

"You've asked for it," Sears said. "You're through."

"I don't think you'll shoot," Jeff said. "I don't think you want to hang, or whatever they do to you in this state."

"No," Sears agreed patiently, "I don't want to hang. I didn't say anything about shooting. I said you were through. Since you won't play ball you can count yourself out. The rest of us have three charts. We don't need you."

Jeff said, "One of you may not even need a map. I seem to remember that there was one here and that it's missing."

Helen saw Nick smile crookedly and put his billfold back in his pocket. Sylvia had closed her handbag; the ice rattled in her glass when she picked up her drink.

"That isn't why you're in such a hell of a hurry, is it?" Jeff asked Sears. "The afternoon's half shot; we couldn't even get well started on a survey. But if I had a full set of directions and I had a map I think I could put 'em down on the map and have a lot of fun tonight."

Buttoning his coat, Sears said quietly, "I think Harry took that map. We'll never know what he did with it. He may also have taken the location papers, but since they're missing it's possible some one else has made a map. I suppose we had better wait until morning," he concurred, and since that ended the matter he went outside for a walk.

Jeff went to Sylvia at the table and she put down her drink and went outside with him. Cole returned to the office to finish a letter so that he could get off to town. Nick poured himself another drink.

"You'd better sit down before you fall down," he said.

Helen did not reply. She again released her grip on the back of the chair and again limped to the foot of the stairs. With the letdown in the tension she had a chance to realize how thoroughly rotten she felt. The walk to Billy Bedrock's had been much too much for her bruised knee, and it was hurting with every step. It was swelling nicely, too. Her chest was sore where the rope had pulled her out of the shaft. Inside she felt completely hollow from her heels to her head. She looked vaguely at Sin standing with folded arms in the doorway of the dining room.

"Damn late for lunch," he said.

Helen shook her head. "I don't want any."

"Why'n hell not?" he asked. He was in a bad humor. "Betta eat, dlink, be melly," he advised. "Tomollow somebody die, like usual."

Helen leaned on the newel post.

"All right," she said. "I'll have a drink."

Sin turned and went to the kitchen. Helen put an arm around the newel post. It was a nice newel post with a big round wooden ball on top you could lean your forehead against. She heard Nick walk over and stop close behind her. It was too much effort to turn her head.

His voice was sympathetic. "Pretty shot, aren't you? Anything I can do?"

Helen thought it over, her forehead resting comfortably against the newel post. She thought over all that he had done. She reached a conclusion.

"You can go to hell," she said wearily.

Nick did not say anything. He continued to stand there until Sin shuffled in from the kitchen. Helen rolled her head to one side on the newel post. She looked at a water glass of pale brown liquid.

"Time Bomb Cocktail," Sin announced. His walnut-shell wrinkles beamed with pride.

Helen unwound her arm from the newel post, took the glass and drank it determinedly.

"Tick-tock," she said, and dragged herself up the stairs and limped down the hall to her room. She had thought she would lie down for a while, but when she looked at hen face in the mirror she decided she'd better do a refinishing job first. She opened a jar of cold cream and began work with a face tissue. She was so tired her fingers began bumping into her nose as she wiped her face. It was unusual and annoying. She hooked her left elbow on top of the bureau, leaning sideways against the bureau, while with her right hand she rubbed in a vanishing cream. She wondered if she were growing a beard? A full, luxuriant beard . . .

She swung around to face the mirror, thrusting her head forward to see better, and she saw that she was rubbing the vanishing cream on top of her head. That was not right. Perhaps she'd better lie down. . . . Then she saw that the bed was a raft on a high sea. She could never swim that far. But it was a nice bed. She whistled to it and it bobbed right around behind her and hit her in back of the knees and she was lying on the bed and it was the Fourth of July and the fireworks she saw with her eyes closed were lovely.

She did not hear the sound of the car when Cole left or when he returned from town near sunset.

Thoughtfully rubbing the back of his scrawny neck, Sin shuffled through the dining room into the kitchen, very clean and neat with a wisp of savory aroma in the air.

Stopping shortly within the door he sniffed the air as if it did not smell good and eyed the kitchen as if it were a shambles. With final, complete disfavor he looked upon John, expertly kneading yeast dough for tomorrow's hot rolls.

Still rubbing the back of his neck, Sin shuffled across the floor on bent knees, like an old man skating on fly-paper, and stopped in front of the yeast dough. Removing his hand from the back of his neck he jabbed a forefinger into the dough, pinched it between forefinger and thumb and wagged his head as a man who has expected to find a mess and has not been disappointed. Again sniffing the air, he went to the wood range and opened the oven. A ham, spiked with cloves and cinnamon sticks, nestling in peaches, was roasting lusciously. He removed two of the cloves and one cinnamon stick and, after jabbing a fork in the ham, went to the woodbox and put another stick of wood in the stove. Again rubbing the back of his neck he slowly skated back into the dining room.

John opened the firebox, removed the smoking piece of wood and tossed it out the back door. He replaced two cloves and a cinnamon stick in the ham. He resumed kneading the dough on the breadboard.

In the dining room Sin felt fairly safe from interruption, deeming it unlikely that his nephew's son in the kitchen would soon seek the company of his great-uncle. He went slowly and quietly about setting the table. The windows of the dining room were open just above the heads of Sylvia and Jay Warren Cole as they sat in two chairs which, earlier, Jeff had drawn back into the shade from the edge of the terrace.

Sylvia said, "You can give me your chart."

Cole's voice was desperately humble. "If you wish," he said. "Anything. Though I can't understand why you want it."

Sylvia's voice was a bitter whisper. "Because then at least," she said, "I'll know you haven't got three of them."

Jeff stepped outside from the lounge.

"Sin's setting the table for dinner," he said. "Hadn't you better call Helen?"

Sylvia found her sitting on the edge of the bed.

"I've just come to," Helen said. "What day is it?" Her next question was unusual. "Am I bald?" she asked.

Sylvia laughed. "Do you feel that bad?"

"No, in fact I seem to feel pretty good. Only I seem to remember rubbing some vanishing cream on the top of my head." She fingered the hair on top of her head. "Time Bomb Cocktail," she said. "Tick-tock, and lights out."

"We've been wondering," Sylvia told her. "Nick asked Sin what was in it." She grinned, quoted in a sing-song that was pretty good, "'Blandy, Jamaica lum, lemon extlact, honey and lye.'"

"Lye?" Helen repeated with interest. She nodded. "I wondered what did it."

Sylvia said with dignity, "Lye whisky."

"You don't know," Helen told her. "You were right the first time." She rose and to her surprise was able to stand.

Sylvia found Nick waiting in his doorway when she started down the hall to her room.

"How's the patient?" he asked.

Sylvia laughed. "She rubbed vanishing cream on top of her head."

Nick stopped smiling. "Too bad it didn't work," he said.

Sylvia continued to smile. "Not had much luck in driving her away, have you? And not much time left."

"You may be right about the time," he said. "If you are, it's time you gave me back the automatic."

Sylvia had put her hand in her handbag when she had joined him at the door. She continued to smile.

"Possession," she said, "is nine points of the law . . . and when it's loaded it's all ten, Nicky dear."

Nick said, "What's happened to us in the last couple days? We liked each other. I think we still do."

"Yes, I think we're suited to each other."

"Even if you didn't feel that way I don't think you'd shoot me."

"In the foot, I would."

Nick looked at her handbag. It was pointed at his foot. He looked into her amber eyes. He locked his hands behind him.

"You're making a mistake not to trust me," he told her.

Sylvia simpered. "Oh, I bet you just say that to all your investors!" It seemed to amuse her as she went on down the hall to her room.

It was a quiet, jittery evening. They played rummy. Helen knew that she was playing like a girl in love but that was because she was thinking about tomorrow. Tomorrow would see the end. She wished it were tomorrow now. They were to get up at dawn. They went to bed around ten o'clock.

As usual, Helen found that she could not get to sleep. The four hours or five she had had that afternoon were only a drop in the bucket to the sleep she had missed since she had been at Dead Finger, but if you wanted to sleep at Dead Finger you wanted to be dead on your feet, not just ready to drop. She kept thinking about tomorrow. About the others who were waiting for tomorrow. They kept going around in her mind like people riding on a wearily grinding merry-go-round that she could not stop watching.

Sears . . . his granite face looked at her expressionlessly as he went by. "I don't want trouble," he said quietly. No one believed that was what he meant. They believed that he meant that he did not want trouble to come into the open. But perhaps . . . Jay Warren Cole was smiling at her blandly, and then as her eyes followed him he was bobbing up and down on his wooden horse like a spider . . . Sylvia, holding the reins in one hand, the other hand hidden in her handbag, Sylvia, looking back over her shoulder at Jeff, a smile on her lips but her almond eyes strangely sad . . . Jeff, his face bruised, its expression baffled and battered, her feeling of being a little less lost and lonely as his eyes met hers, a sense of something lost when his eyes turned again to Sylvia. . . . Then Nick. Nick—

The merry-go-round stopped, vanished, at the crash of a shot.

Helen was standing in her bare feet at the side of her bed. Inside? Outside? Cringing against the wall, she peered out the window opening to the back of the lodge. She froze as she saw a dark figure scramble into a bedroom window. It would be . . . Nick's bedroom.

Helen banged into the bed, jerked the chair from under the doorknob and opened the door. The dark hall stopped her cold. She heard some one calling. It sounded like Cole. She heard another door open. She quickly closed hers, ran to the bed, the bedside table, fumbled for matches on the table, lit the oil lamp, carried it back with her to the door.

At the far end of the hall Sylvia was holding a lamp in the doorway of her bedroom. Her father was facing her in the doorway of his. Nick was going down the hall towards them. Jeff's door opened and flung more light into the hall from a lamp burning on his bedside table. Helen joined the parade. Sylvia advanced to meet them, Cole trailing her.

"It's all right," she said. Her voice was calm. She looked calm. The lamp was steady in her left hand, there was something casual but competent in the way her right hand was holding the automatic. "It's quite all right," she insisted. "I'm sorry to have awakened you."

"What the hell was it?" Jeff asked. He was far from composed.

"Some one tried to crawl through my window," Sylvia said. Her amber gaze went to Nick's face. "I missed him," she said.

Helen looked at Nick's face. He was white with anger. He was breathing hard. There was a tear over one knee of his pajamas. Helen saw that Jeff was taking in the way Nick and Sylvia were looking at each other. She saw Jeff's face began to set, like concrete. Helen leaned against the wall.

"Impossible," Cole was repeating, "impossible."

"Oh, no," Sylvia said. "Quite easy, really. The edge of the embankment is only two or three feet from the wall and nearly as high as this floor. Don't you think it would be quite easy?" she asked Nick.

"Impossible!" Cole repeated more firmly. "It's impossible to believe that any one would dare, would think of—"

"That's not very flattering, father," Sylvia objected. She continued to look at Nick. "But I've no doubt," she said, "that it was just a business and not a social call."

Nick said, "So that's why you shot."

Helen saw Jeff's elbow swing back. Nick was still looking at Sylvia when the fist struck the side of his jaw. Helen had watched the blow start but she was not prepared for the loudness of the sound it made. Her mouth sagged open at the brutal thud of it. She stood sagging against the wall, breathing through her mouth, the lamp held at a rigid but acute angle in her hand.

Nick was slammed back sideways in a crash against the door of Sears' bedroom. The door banged open at the impact. Nick sprawled in a half-sitting position against the doorjamb, his knee ripping through the tear in his pajamas. He shook his head, trying to clear his eyes.

Looking down at him, Jeff thrust out his hand to Sylvia.

"Give me the gun," he said. "By God, if there's another occasion I won't miss."

Sylvia was looking at Nick. His eyes met hers.

"Perhaps that's why I shot, Nick," she said. "And perhaps it's why I missed." Still looking at him she held out the automatic to Jeff.

Nick suddenly realized where he was sitting.

"Where's Sears?" he asked.

Helen wanted to laugh. Not for a second or two. It was a little too much to digest instantly. It had been in her mind all evening, of course. In all their minds. If some one had her chart and Harry McIntyre's, that would, with his own, make three charts. If any one had three charts and a map he would have to get away with the gold tonight, before they found it together tomorrow. But that it had happened, and that it was Sears, that the nightmare was ended, it took a second or two to take it in because it was too good to be true.

Jeff charged into the bedroom.

Nick said viciously, "Under the bed, no doubt." He looked up at Sylvia. "If I'd had the gun, I'd have kept guard tonight!"

Sylvia did not answer. Helen at first thought that Sylvia was looking at her, that she was smiling because she, too, was feeling a blessed release; and then she saw that Sylvia was looking past her, up the hall. Helen turned her head but could not see beyond the smoking lamp in her hand. She straightened the lamp, held it higher.

George Sears was standing at the head of the stairs. He was not in nightclothes. He was fully dressed. Jeff charged back into the hall, stepping over Nick, stopped short at the sight of Sears. Sears took his hand from the revolver in his belt and, buttoning his coat, came down the hall.

"I was afraid there'd been some trouble," he said.

Jeff was white. "Where the hell have you been?"

"For a walk."

"With charts and a map," Jeff said. "And what's that in your coat pocket? It's the steel tape, isn't it? By God, this is the showdown."

The automatic was steady and level. Helen felt how very still Sears had become as he stood beside her. She saw how ugly Jeff's face had become, white, twisted. He's maddened, she thought. *Maddened because of Sylvia and Nick.* She saw Nick draw up his foot to kick. He, too, knew that Jeff was ready to kill.

"Jeff!" she cried, but did not hear the word for the crash of the shot.

The automatic lay on the floor ten feet down the hall. Helen continued to look at where it had been in Jeff's hand, where now the skin was stripped from the finger he had had around the trigger and blood dripped to the floor.

Bent half double, Sin shuffled in from the landing of the outside stairs. His carbine was at his shoulder and it was pointed at Sears' head.

"Take out gun," he said.

Sears slowly unbuttoned his coat. Holding the right lapel with his right hand he pulled the coat open. Very slowly he reached his left hand across his body, thumb and forefinger extended. With thumb and forefinger he gingerly took hold of the grip of the revolver and, by pulling in his stomach, loosened the pressure enough to draw it out. He slowly extended it at arm's length that way in front of him.

Sin said, "Dlop." Sears dropped it. "Kickee," Sin instructed. Sears put the toe of his shoe against it and slid it down the floor to him. The carbine swung around to Jeff.

"Kickee Colt down heah." Jeff was holding his torn hand. "Hully up." Jeff went to the automatic and gave it a shove with his bare foot. It went as far as Sears. Sears relayed it. Sin switched the carbine to one hand, holding it like a pistol. He was so far bent over that he did not have to stoop much more to pick up the revolver and automatic and tuck them under the satin sash-belt of his cerise pajamas.

"Now maybe get some sleep some night," he said, and with that farewell he shuffled back to the landing and down the stairs.

Sears looked at Jeff. He looked at him for a long time; he slowly turned his back and went to the door of his room. Nick was getting to his feet. When he got out of Sears' way Sears went into the room and closed the door. Cole watched Sylvia go to Jeff. He looked vaguely, as if lost, at Nick and Helen and then turned away and went to his room.

"Better come down to the kitchen where we can get some hot water," Sylvia was saying to Jeff. "Is it broken?"

"I guess not," he said. "I can move it."

They went to the stairs. Helen slowly slid down the wall, careful of the lamp, and set the lamp on the floor when she sat on the floor. She was glad she was wearing pajamas. She could cross her feet in front of her and hook her hands over her spread knees and let her forehead sink forward upon her forearms and the hell with it. The hell with it, with everything, just let her rest. Snuggling her head on one side on her crossed arms she saw Nick follow Sylvia and Jeff downstairs. The hell with it. Then, just as she was getting really settled and comfortable, she saw Nick come up again. He was carrying a couple of glasses. He sat down beside her and put one of the glasses in her hand. She didn't know if it were worth while sitting up for a Scotch but try anything once. She tried it. It was worth it.

Nick had lit a cigarette. He handed it to her. Lit another for himself. The drink and the cigarette were so much what she needed that Helen could have cried.

"If only you weren't such a bastard," she said. She began to realize that she was crying. "You louse," she said. "Make me cry when I'm so tired. You dirty louse."

She threw the Scotch and soda in his face, threw the cigarette after it, stumbled to her feet and limped down the hall to her room. She slammed the door, threw herself down on the bed and went to sleep.

Jeff was down late for breakfast. It had been slow work dressing with his right hand swollen to half again its normal size. While he ate, and the rest of them waited for him in the lounge, Helen stepped outside on the terrace. In the blue light of the dawn the world was cool and clean.

When Nick joined her she said, "I'm sorry about last night. I was a little beast."

"It's all right," Nick said. "I haven't laughed so much since . . . I wouldn't have minded it at all if I hadn't suspected that another man caused it."

Helen did not want to take that up, not any part of it.

"How do your eyes feel?" she asked. "They look inflamed."

Sears' voice was flat and hard from the doorway.

"Come here," he said.

Sears and Cole were no place in sight when they entered the lounge. Jeff was standing in the office doorway. He stepped inside and they followed him. Sears was jerking open the drawers of the desk. Cole was rummaging in a corner. Sylvia was standing by the tripod of the transit looking down at an open, green-felt-lined, empty wood case.

"It's gone," she said tonelessly. "The telescope thing."

Cole kicked a rolled window shade out of his way. "While we were waiting," he said, "we thought we'd get things ready. Came in for the transit. When I picked up the case I knew something was wrong."

Sears came forward from the desk.

"This searching is senseless," he said. "It hasn't been misplaced," he continued quietly. "It's been stolen."

Helen thought, *It's been stolen so that we can't survey today. Some one has taken it and dropped it down a shaft so that we'll be held here another day. Another night. In this trap. She knew that they were all thinking that.* They all knew that all of them were thinking that. There was no use in talking about it.

Nick said, "I'll drive in and see if I can scare up another one. Harry got this at the land office?"

Cole nodded. "They may not be able to spare another. But some one else should have one."

"You'd better come in with me. Two can cover more ground than one."

Sears said, "If you can make a quick enough trip—" he broke off, looking out the window.

They filed out into the lounge as Billy Bedrock came in from the terrace. He exchanged good mornings with Helen, gave a general smile to the others.

"I was wondering if you happened to be intending to go in to town today?" he asked.

"By an odd coincidence," Nick said, "we do happen to be going in though we hadn't intended to."

Billy looked happy. "Would it trouble you to take me along?"

"Not at all."

"Well, that's fine! Little something I'd like to send off to the assay office." He winked. "You could guess."

Nick said, "I've been doing some guessing."

"Well," Billy said happily, "I'm glad I'm in time to go with you."

"Just in time," Nick said. "By another odd coincidence, we seldom leave before sunrise, but this morning you're just exactly in time."

He gave Helen a look from which she turned away. She stood in the doorway while they went out to the car, waved to Billy as the car passed in front of the lodge on the terrace.

"I think I'll have some more coffee," she said to Jeff. Sylvia and Sears had strolled with the others to the car, had not yet walked back. "I think I can use a lot of coffee," she said.

Jeff sat down with her. When she stirred her coffee it sounded to her as if she were playing a snare drum. She shook the spoon out of the cup and rattled it down on the saucer. There was no sense in trying to pick up the cup. She clasped her hands in her lap.

"Must be the wages of a misspent youth," she said. "I don't seem to be conditioned for this sort of party." The way Jeff was looking at her made wisecracking out of order. "I guess it just took all I had to keep from jumping in the car," she explained. "With my trunk, I mean."

Jeff shook a cigarette out of a package with his left hand, lit it with his left hand.

"I'm glad I'm durable," he said. His swollen and bandaged right hand, his bruised face and bandaged forehead, gave substance to his words. "If memory serves," he went on, "I was the first person here to have an accident. Even lived through a second one. Gives me hopes of surviving if I'm picked for the next one."

Tension was a peculiar thing, Helen thought. After a while you got the jitters only when there was a letdown. When it was turned on again you were yourself again. She picked up her cup with a steady hand and, in bravado, cocked her little finger. She wondered why she had never done it before, it looked cute out there.

There was not any bravado in her voice.

"So you think that's what it means, too," she said, "the transit thing being gone?"

Jeff said, "I think some one needs more time. If another accident's needed to stop us, to give more time, I think there'll be another."

Helen took a sip of coffee. She decided to say it.

"If there's another one," she said, "we'll know it's murder. I won't keep my mouth shut about murder."

"I wish you'd go, Helen. I wish to God you'd go."

Helen took another sip of coffee. "What about Sylvia?" she asked.

"She has her father here." He saw what she was thinking. "All right," he said, "and she hasn't a cut in what we're after and so there won't be any difference in what's left for the rest of us. I guess you're right. You'd be a fool to believe that I was only thinking about you."

Helen smiled wanly. "I wish it were as simple as that," she said. "I wish I could completely mistrust you."

"Or—Nick?"

"Or Nick," she admitted. "It's what makes it horrible. To know that either of you can be so darned nice, and mean it, and yet that feeling that way you still might . . ."

Sylvia and Sears came into the lounge and then into the dining room.

Sears said, "Miss Cole and I have been having a little talk. She doesn't like this delay. I don't like it. I don't think you do. There's a chance we can do something about it."

Sylvia opened her handbag, took out a folded piece of white linen. "I had my father give me his chart," she explained.

Helen thought, *And Nick feeling so safe because he has Cole with him!* At any other time she would have laughed.

Sears said to Jeff, "With mine and yours that gives us three."

Jeff looked puzzled. "I don't see where that gets us without a map."

Sears said, "I have a map."

9

Helen was raising her coffee cup to her lips. She heard George Sears say, "I have a map." The cup was at her lips. She took a sip of it. She lowered it nearly to its saucer and then raised it again, slowly, to prolong the excuse that it gave her not to look at the others. She needed a moment to herself to fathom the meaning of his announcement. She heard with indifference Jeff repeat, "You have a map?" and Sears reply, "It's one I made." The fact that he was in possession of a map was no surprise to her. It was his admission of the fact. It took her a moment to realize why that had been such a shock to her. It was because that admission implied his innocence. If he had three charts he would have everything to lose and nothing to gain by admitting that he had a map. She had not known how much she had been counting upon George Sears to be the possessor of three charts, how much she had been counting upon it being George Sears and not one of the other men . . .

"It's one you made?" Jeff repeated. "From the location papers?" he asked. It was just a question. It did not sound as if he were hunting for trouble.

"No," Sears said. "I've had to trust to memory and pacing off some of the lines. You and Miss Cole watched me from the terrace yesterday afternoon."

"Yes," Jeff said, "we saw you ambling around in circles." If his words were a polite way of calling Sears a liar, his tone had a note of dangerous anger.

Sylvia said persuasively, "But once in a while he went in a very straight line. That's why I thought he might be working on a map. It's why I spoke to him about it now," she explained, and Jeff seemed to accept it. Her voice went down to a whisper. "I can't face another night here," she pleaded. "Let's use his map. Try to find the gold, now." She turned desperately for an ally. "Helen, you, don't you want to end this, not another night, end it now?"

Helen could have screamed her reply. "Yes," she said.

Sylvia turned back to Jeff.

"All right," Jeff agreed.

"I'll get the map," Sears said. He left the dining room.

They waited for him in the office and they waited in silence. Jeff dusted off one end of a long draftsman's table with his handkerchief, kept on dusting at it. Sylvia picked up the white window shade from where Cole had kicked it to one side in his hunt for the transit. Taking all the time possible she neatly and tightly rolled it up and set it back in the corner. Helen simply waited, watching Jeff dust the table, watching Sylvia roll up the hacked-edged window shade from which Saul Baron had cut the seven charts. She waited and kept her secret.

Sears did not keep them waiting long. When he came in he took some of Cole's business envelopes from the desk, tore off the flaps, and pasted the map to the drafting table. Cleanly ruled lines made adjoining quadrilaterals. He pointed out that not all of the forty-odd claims were oblong parallelograms like so many dominoes. Billy Bedrock had staked his two original claims over a half mile apart, and when it had come to filling in the intervening land, and avoiding certain claims of Mr. Parsons to which he had had an incontestable title, it had been necessary to cut a good many of the dominoes to fit.

"I think I have the boundaries right," he said. "I once knew them by heart. Other things I remember check up, the locations of shafts, tunnels, conveyor towers, things like that. But if my memory's off, the map could be badly off. I want you to understand that."

Jeff thought it over. "You won't mind my mentioning," he said, "that this could be a build-up for a letdown."

Sears did not seem to take offense.

"No," he said, "I don't mind you mentioning it. Not now, before we use the map, if we do use it. I don't want trouble. Before we start it must be understood and agreed that this map may be wrong. I don't think it is. I'm willing to give it a try, now, because the sooner we find the gold the less chance there is for trouble. But I don't want trouble if the map is wrong."

Sylvia unfolded an oblong of linen and put it beside the map. They stood looking at it, open to be read: *CHART . . . No. 6*. Sylvia stood looking at Jeff.

"All right," he decided.

Helen, her lips tight, watched Jeff spread out CHART No. 4 and Sears line up CHART No. 3. She thought: *If this had been done on the night we found them, Mr. Parsons and Harry McIntyre would still be alive. Or if she had had sense enough to keep her mouth shut about finding a chart in the first place. At least she had learned enough to keep her mouth shut now.*

"The scale's twenty feet to the thirty-second," Sears was saying. He opened a pocket magnifying glass. "No matter how carefully we work our margin of error is not going to be in inches."

No, not in inches, Helen thought. *And certainly not in error.*

Jeff said, "I'm not worried about that part of it."

"If we can get within a hundred feet," Sears agreed, "I'm not worried about finding it. I think Saul would put it where he could get at it at night. That means a land-mark." He looked at Helen. "That's how I happened to see you at work with the cord the night Harry was killed," he said. "I'd noticed that the shafthead was in line with the end of the survey."

Helen wondered why, now, he was reminding her that he had found the cord. Was he trying to get over the idea that if he had been at the shafthead he had not been on the dump of Sourdough, had not murdered Harry McIntyre? But why, now, was he reminding her that some one had been on the dump of Sourdough? Was he warning her to be on guard against some one? The only other man there was Jeff.

Sears had turned back to the map.

"My Starting Direction," he continued evenly, "is 1200 feet at 35 degrees from the baseline. Will you all check that?"

Five hours later they knew that they were nowhere. They had been suspecting as much for some time. The pen-cil dot on the map had been easily located in the field. It had been within a hundred feet of the southeastern corner of New Discovery claim, marked in the field by a brass-topped lead-pipe survey post. The post was located over a mile from the lodge, over the top of the eastern ridge, at the foot of a hundred-foot cliff, in the middle of a shale slide about a thousand feet long. Since there was no tell-ing what day the cliff might add a thousand tons of rock to the slide it seemed an unlikely place for Saul Baron to have buried gold that, at the time, he had had every hope of recovering.

But at the edge of the slide there was a prospect hole some six feet deep. They had come prepared for digging and the hole was seven feet deep by the time it was scraped clean of muck to the living rock. The weathered mound, with grass sprouting from what seemed bare rock, that was where the dump of the hole had been attacked with more anticipation than the hole itself. To hide a hole under the worthless dump of another hole would be a shrewd way to guard it against chance discovery. With that thought, the dump had been moved with pick, shovel and bare hands. There was nothing under it but living rock.

Jeff put down the shovel and began putting on his shirt.

"How long would it take to check the map?" he asked.

"This is an end claim," Sears explained. "End of property. The interior claims don't have these survey posts at their corners with the exception of the northeast-southeast ones of Gold Pocket which we used as a baseline in laying out the other claims. Without the location papers there's no way on earth to check the map."

It's going to come now, Helen thought, *the explosion that's been hanging fire between them. She would have to speak now.*

But Sylvia said, desperately, "We knew the map might be wrong, Jeff."

"Yes," Jeff said. "Yes, I knew." He picked up the shovel. "Let's forget it."

Sylvia said what they all were thinking: "What shall we tell Nick?"

"Let's forget it," Jeff repeated. "Since we didn't find anything, let's just forget it." He looked at Helen.

She did not need to speak. She knew that her face showed her relief.

Sears nodded. "I don't want trouble," he agreed. He took the map out of his pocket, struck a match and put it to the map. "One thing less to cause trouble," he said.

He got drunk that night. He did not begin until late afternoon when Nick and Cole returned from town. They

did not have a transit with them. The three general stores
in Sasoon did not have a very lively business in transits. If
a dry farmer wanted to put up a fence he did it by guess
and by God; if a rancher wanted to string out a few miles
of line he avoided arguments by hiring a surveyor from
the land office, and that was the trouble: the land-office
surveyor and the remaining land-office transit were busy
over on the other side of the valley. Willet Price had tried
to be helpful. There was a rancher fifteen miles from town
who was reported to have a mail-order surveyor's level.
He still had it because one of his children had lost the
eye-piece. When they had got back to town they had tele-
phoned to Tucson and a transit would arrive in Sasoon the
next morning.

It was after the receipt of this news that Sears began
drinking. He drank in silence. There is a difference between a man who is not talking and one who is silent.

Helen found that it was a threatening, depressing difference. She saw that she was not the only one. And not
only Sylvia but the men as well glanced uneasily at him
as he sat after dinner staring at the fire and pouring rye
into his pock-marked face. It was fairly late before he let
them go to bed. That was what it amounted to. Tired as
they were they did not take to the idea of lying awake in
their rooms wondering what he might do. It was a distinct
surprise when, at the end, all that he did was to lurch to
his feet and sway upstairs to his room.

Sylvia crawled out of her chair.

"A very good idea," she said. "I wish I'd thought of it
first."

"'Sleep,'" Jay Warren Cole affirmed, also rising, "'that
knits up the ravell'd sleave of care.' A very excellent idea."

Sylvia turned at the foot of the stairs. "I meant getting
drunk," she said. "I wish I were stinking, blotto drunk."

Cole was deprecatory. "My dear child . . ."

Sylvia spoke to him alone, "Too drunk to think," she said. "Too drunk to care." She went on up the stairs.

No one looked at Cole as he followed her. Helen moved to the chair that Sears had vacated close beside the fire. Her hands and feet were cold. She did not look at either Jeff or Nick until she turned her head to answer Jeff's good night. Jeff's footsteps went up the stairs. She heard the clink of glass at the table.

"You might fix me one," she said. "If you please." Nick brought her a Scotch, set his own on the mantel. He said, "I'd got the impression you were on the wagon this evening."

"It sticks in my throat when I see any one pouring it down as he was."

Nick hooked his elbow on the mantel.

"I'm disappointed in Red," he said. "I thought he could take it."

"Some of us have taken a good deal," she said. "Perhaps it's easier for whoever's dishing it out." She unhurriedly sipped at her glass, but her drink was half gone before he spoke again.

"I'm tired of telling you that you're a fool," he said. "A gold-crazy fool to stay here."

Her mind agreed with him that she was a fool for staying. She had found it bad enough to stay while her mind had told her heart that she was a fool for staying, but she had not known what bitterness really was until she heard his opinion of her staying.

She said, "You know everything. Understand all."

The lamp was on the table some distance away, to one side, in back of him. The light from the fire brought out a hard line of jaw, a curl of lower lip, a beak of nose, a gleam of black hair. *Perhaps he looks too much like a savage,* Helen thought. *Perhaps he's too obvious. Perhaps that's his disguise. Perhaps I've been an even blinder fool than he thinks.*

"I can tell you one thing I know," he said. "All the gold you're going to get out of this . . ." He let it go at that.

Helen said, "I see. After we find it you're going to cheat me out of my share?"

"So after all this," he said, "you still think that we're all going to find it together before some one person finds it alone?"

"Suppose you tell me," she suggested.

Nick Baron took his glass from the mantel but did not drink.

"I've tried to get you out of it," he said, as if to himself. Then he directly faced her. "I don't want you to get hurt."

Helen looked as if her drink tasted bad.

"It's not because you want to get me out of the way," she said.

"I can't help you if you won't believe me."

Helen closed her eyes.

"You have a heart of gold," she said. "You've been working it overtime. It must be tired. Good-night."

She heard the glass set back on the mantel. There was only a slight pause before his footsteps went to the stairs, mounted the stairs; a door closed upstairs. She rose and put another log on the fire where it would burn low but long. She kicked off her shoes and snuggled down in the leather-cushioned chair, her glass on one of the oak arms, cigarettes and matches on the other. She smoked a cigarette and finished her Scotch, her eyelids heavy in the warm firelight. She made herself a little more comfortable. The light in the room gave a soothing sense of security. She thought that she was still gazing into the flicker of the fire when she went to sleep.

Sears also was sleeping. His heavy, drunken breathing gave, he thought, good evidence that he was asleep. He did not try to overdo it. Deliberate breathing is hard labor. It was enough to give a half snore in about one breath in ten.

Even that became tiresome enough in time, and there was no telling how long he might have to keep it up.

He was glad that time does not mean too much after the better part of a quart of rye. He was pleased that none of those remaining at the lodge knew how liquor effected him. He had not had to simulate his lurch to his feet or his swaying progress up the stairs. Anything over a pint made him unsteady. But by some trick of nerves his bull of a body took the punishment and left his mind unbefuddled. Harry McIntyre, his constant companion for ten years, would have known that the one thing liquor never did to him was to make him sleepy, but Harry was out of the way and the others did not know.

The door was opened so quietly that, with his head turned towards the window, his first warning of its opening was the draft that swept over the bed from the window to the hall. When the draft stopped he knew that the door was closed again. At the creak of a floorboard near the bed he sat up and switched on the flashlight that he had been holding in his hand.

"You're late, Jay," he said. "I've been waiting a couple of hours."

In the beam of the flashlight Cole's round face was a pasty disk. He raised a hand in front of his eyes, tried to step aside from the blinding light, stopped when he knocked over a chair.

Sears said, "I expected you to come through the window, along the first-floor roof from your window. The door, I thought for a moment it must be some one else." His voice was a little thick, but quiet, conversational. "I was surprised," he continued, "that anybody else had been so clever." He swung his feet to the floor. "Depend on you to think of things first, Jay."

Cole dropped his hand from in front of his eyes when the circle of light was lowered to focus on his round belly. His red silk dressing gown reflected the light in a rosy glow in which he was able to see Sears sitting on the edge of the bed, fully dressed, waiting for him to speak as patiently as he had waited for him to come to the room.

Cole said, "I was going to awaken you. There's something I think we should discuss."

"About the survey," Sears said.

"Yes," Cole admitted. "Sylvia told me. And I've been wondering—" he stopped as the light was switched off.

There was a crack of light under the door. Some one had a lamp in the hall. Sears lurched to his feet, his hand falling heavily on Cole's shoulder.

"In a half hour," he whispered. "Downstairs."

"Miss Farr's there. Asleep."

"Outside, then."

"Where?" Cole asked.

"In the car."

Sears pushed him towards the window and went to the door. Swinging it open, he swayed out into the hall and blinked owlishly at Sylvia, who was standing with a lamp in one hand and the other on the doorknob of her father's room, the adjoining room.

"Thank you," Sears said gravely. "Thank you for the light."

She did not reply but she continued to stand there until he found the bathroom door. When he came out the hall was dark except at the stairs to the lounge and for a crack of light under Sylvia's bedroom door. Since it was behind her door instead of Cole's he assumed that his appearance in the hall had turned her from taking a look in her father's room, or if she had he had delayed her long enough for Cole to get back in bed. She must have heard the chair upset and thought that the sound came from her father's room.

Sears stood it up again and sat down in it. After a quarter of an hour he cautiously opened his door. There was no longer a crack of light under Sylvia's. He waited another ten minutes and then went down the outside stairway.

The car was parked in an open-front shed set back against the embankment left by the blasting out of the terrace. The three walls and the roof were enough to blot out the light of the quarter moon, low in the sky. Sears thought that he was the first to arrive until Cole spoke to him from the darkness of the front seat.

"Here, Red."

Sears got in behind the steering wheel.

"Be careful of the horn."

"We don't want company," Sears agreed. "We don't need any one else."

Cole sucked in his breath.

"The survey this afternoon was really very fortunate," he said. "I imagine you have a good memory for figures."

Sears said, "I may be able to remember a couple of angles and distances." He stirred impatiently. "Why beat around the bush? You sneaked into my room to see if you could find a map. All right, I have a map. And you have a chart."

Cole said, "If we can work together . . ."

"You've a chart," Sears cut him short, "or you wouldn't have come looking for a map. Stop beating around the bush. I don't want trouble."

Cole said, "I have a chart."

"With you?"

"No," Cole said quickly. "In a safe place. A very safe place."

"Where?"

Cole's voice was reluctant. "In the lodge."

"Then get it. We'll get to work now." Cole was silent. "Get it," Sears repeated quietly.

Cole shifted his weight, opened the door of the car.

Helen sat up, wide awake, too startled for an instant to realize what it was that had awakened her. It was outside— the motor of the car, a clash of gears. She rose, ran to the door opening on the terrace. As she reached the door the headlights of the car flashed in front of the lodge. She stepped back inside the doorway as they swept towards her, ran out on the terrace when they were passed.

The car tore down the road. Helen heard shouts inside the lodge. The headlights of the car swung from side to side. They picked up the stampmill. Helen's mouth opened as the car plunged down upon the sharp turn around the ridge. She did not cry out. Impossibly, the car made the turn.

Jeff came running out of the lodge in his pajamas. He nearly ran into her, grasped her arm.

"Who was it?" he shouted.

Helen said, "He made the turn. I don't know how."

Jeff shook her arm. "Who was it?"

"I don't know."

Jeff looked towards the doorway. "Who was it?" he asked.

"Sears," Nick said, joining them. "Jay looked in his room. The rest of us are here."

Sylvia paused in the doorway.

"He was drunk," she said. "He'll kill himself."

Nick said, "I don't know how drunk he was."

"I saw him in the hall," she explained, joining them. "About a half hour ago. He was reeling."

"And we fell for it," Jeff said. "Fell for an act."

Helen shook her head. "You didn't see him drive down the road," she said. "He barely stayed on. It's only a miracle he made the turn."

"My God," Jeff said. "Don't you know what's happened? I've been played for a damn fool, but at least I know it now."

Helen looked at Sylvia, moved to her side.

"The map," she said. She put her arm around Sylvia.

"My God, at last," Jeff said.

Helen and Sylvia were looking at Nick.

"What's this about a map?" he asked.

Helen said, "He had a map he'd made. Sylvia had her father's chart. We marked out the directions on the map this morning." Nick was no longer looking at her. He was looking at Jeff. "We didn't find anything," she went on doggedly. "We ended up nowhere."

Nick was still looking at Jeff.

"I knew I was being a damned fool," Jeff said, his voice thick with anger. "I knew the map might be a fake to get a full set of directions. Damn it, don't you think I knew he might have another one!" He stopped trying to defend himself to himself. "But I took the chance," he admitted.

Nick said, "And he's making his getaway with a quarter million dollars in gold."

Helen's arm tightened around Sylvia.

"Thank God," she said. "Thank God it's over."

Nick was saying, "Thirty miles to town. By the time we could walk there, he'd be several hours across the border."

A crash of glass turned their heads. Cole was standing at the table in the lounge. He had stopped for a drink. He began pouring another one.

Sylvia said, "And all that he said to me when I told him about the survey was that I'd been foolish. And now I've caused him to lose . . ." she was halfway to the door to join her father when Nick said:

"What's that?"

They looked where he was looking. Down the mountain, over the ridge, there was a red glow in the sky. They stood looking at the red glow and thinking of one explanation that kept them silent. For the first time since she had been standing outside Helen felt the cold of the rock under her stocking feet. She felt it clear up to the top of her head. She saw Nick start down the road.

Helen turned to the lodge. "I've got to get my shoes," she said to no one in particular.

Cole was still standing at the table. He was splashing another drink into a glass as if he meant to pour out the bottle.

"There's a fire," Helen told him. "It may be down the road." She went on to the fireplace and picked up her shoes. Sylvia stumbled up the stairs in haste, losing a mule from a bare foot; not pausing to pick it up.

"Wait, Helen!"

"Yes."

She did not have long to wait, holding out her hands to coals which did not seem able to warm them, before Sylvia came back down the stairs in sports shoes, a coat over her pajamas.

Helen said, "Your father followed Jeff and Nick."

Sin was waiting on the terrace in hobnailed boots and flowered pajamas, the carbine in the crook of his arms. He gave parting directions to John before following the two girls down the road.

"Build up log fiah. Make plenty coffee. Get flesh bottle lye. All same last time," he concluded.

On the road down to the stampmill Helen could not see the red glow in the sky. It was just a beautiful night with a sliver of moon and cold, clean air. The occasional rattle of a stone reminded that Sin was in back. At her side Sylvia walked like a person alone. There was neither sight nor sound of those ahead.

It was a half mile from the stampmill before Helen saw them. There was the steep ridge, the narrow road a curving shelf, and then it was the place where Mr. Parsons had once set off a dynamite blast. It was redly, waveringly lit up by the burning car and the burning tree a hundred feet below the road. It was an ancient juniper tree, barrel-like in its squat girth, against which the car had shattered itself. It burned like a barrel of oil and firecrackers.

Jay Warren Cole was sitting on the edge of the road staring at the fire. Fifty feet below the burning tree and the burning wreckage of the car Nick Baron was standing beside a ledge of rock. He was taking off his dressing gown. He spread it over something lying against the ledge. Beside him, Jeff suddenly turned away and began climbing back up to the road. Nick followed.

Helen came to a stop beside Cole. Sylvia stood behind him. He did not turn his head. His round face was beaded with perspiration. He did not turn his head when Jeff and Nick came up the road. Jeff was holding a wallet, some letters.

Sin was the first to speak.

"Who'n hell pay this joylide?" he demanded.

"It's all right, Sin," Nick said. "We'll buy you another car."

Cole rose so suddenly that it was startling after his complete immobility. He swung around to face them, turning his back on the fire, and in the light of the quarter moon his moist face looked like the white round belly of a weakfish. The squeamish thing was that he seemed to be trying to smile.

"A drunken whim," he said, his mouth twitching. "It's the only explanation of the terrible accident. A drunken whim."

Nick said, "Somebody's got to get to town. Is there a trail that's shorter than the road?"

Cole's smile slowly stopped twitching. "Over the other side of the ridge," he waved vaguely. "Save ten miles—Mr. Parsons—but I don't know the trail."

Sin said, "Billy know."

Helen jerked away from them. She said, over her shoulder, "I'll get Billy." She walked fast to get away from the work they would be doing. There was blood on Jeff's hands. He had searched the body. Next they would huddle around the wallet, pry through his papers for his chart, for a map. Then, when it was cold enough to draw near, they would poke into the wreckage of the car, poke and pry for gold. She walked fast until she was out of sight of them and she continued to walk fast when a look over her shoulder showed her that Sin was not following her but had stayed on guard behind.

A half mile to the stampmill and then the trail above the gulch, the gulch a black river in the silver night, as silent as the night, and the night was so silent that after a time she could not even hear herself think. That was fine. It was like a nice new life to stop thinking about anything and walk beside a black river in a silver night.

She walked as fast as she could in safety on the trail, and stopped about twenty feet in front of Billy's cabin. The door was open. She called his name. She wished the night were not so silent and called again quickly, going closer to the doorway. She stood in the doorway.

"Billy! . . . Billy!"

Helen Farr closed her mouth tight. It was crazy to lose her head and shout so that the ravine echoed. She remembered the location of his bunk. She went to it. It was empty. She ran out of the cabin, stopping with a scream when Billy spoke to her.

"I'm sorry to have scared you," he said gently. "I've been sleeping out lately," he explained, with a vague motion of his hand towards the head of the ravine.

Helen said, "There's been another accident."

"Yes, Miss?"

"Mr. Sears," Helen said. "He drove the car off the road, near where Mr. Parsons used to work. He's been killed."

Billy shook his head. His white hair was silver mist in the moonlight.

"He built that road himself," he said.

"Some one must go to town," Helen explained. "The car's wrecked. But Mr. Cole says that there's a trail that you know—"

Billy smiled, patted her arm reassuringly.

"I'll be happy," he said, "to go to town for you and tell them he's dead."

Helen turned to start back on the trail to the gulch. Billy stopped her.

"If it's up to Mr. Parsons'," he said, "there's a short cut I always take." He waved his hand towards the head of the ravine.

10

Helen watched the car run down the road and turn out of sight at the stampmill. She heard Nick say:

"Sensible officer, Nordice. No unnecessary fuss."

Willet Price's voice had the sound of sandpaper. "You can thank your reputation," he said. "It's Sasoon's opinion that you're having a drunken orgy up here. That explains everything."

"It explains Sears," Nick said.

The afternoon sun was hot. She felt it hot against her face and through her clothes, but she felt cold. She felt more cold than when she had stood on the terrace the night before.

"It explains everything," Price repeated. "But it's fortunate a drunk can always make every turn but the last one. It's fortunate he made the turn at the mill. A dead man couldn't do that."

"A dead man?"

It was Cole's voice. Helen knew that it was Cole's voice not because it sounded like the voice of Jay Warren Cole, which it did not, but because it sounded like something shaking out of gelatin. He had caught a chill the night before. He had been drinking steadily since and it had neither made him drunk nor helped the chill.

Price said, "You're not the only people who have a reputation. It's common knowledge that before Saul was arrested he deposited twenty thousand dollars in Sin's name. Legally the money is Sin's. He hasn't had to live here on his own savings all these years. He could have pulled out and taken the twenty thousand with him at any time. But he waited for Saul. That's given him something of a reputation for loyalty to Saul." He paused, and then added dryly, "Harry McIntyre and George Sears helped send Saul to prison."

Helen looked at Jay Warren Cole, who also had helped send Saul to prison. His face was something bloated, with whiskers. She looked away from him. She looked down the road so that she did not have to look at any of their faces. But no matter where she looked she saw Sin and was afraid for him.

"This is an entirely new idea to Jay," Nick explained with undisguised sarcasm. "It's never, never, occurred to him before that a dead man could be put in a car and the car started down a road."

"It's fortunate," Price repeated, "that he didn't run off the road before making the turn at the mill." His voice was as dry as unslaked lye. "It's fortunate," he said, "for all of you. Because if there'd been any question, even any possibility, of this not having been an accident I'd have told Nordice all that I know about your reason for being here."

Helen turned from the road, facing him.

"Don't you think I would have!" she said furiously.

Without waiting for a reply she stalked into the lodge. Jeff was sitting at the cold fireplace in the chair in which she had gone to sleep the night before. He looked up heavily, said heavily:

"I thought he'd never leave."

Helen stopped at the foot of the stairs.

"Don't you think we owed him a lunch?" she asked. "After such a nice visit, with no embarrassing questions!"

Jeff looked at her torpidly. "You'll feel better when you get some sleep," he said. "That's the trouble with all of us. We're too tired to see that this . . . auto accident . . . it puts a different light on things."

"Yes!" Helen snapped. "Oh, yes! I'm too tired to see that."

Jeff said wearily, "We know it was an accident. That's the whole point. We can stop imagining things about the other accidents."

"Oh, yes!" Helen said. "I can stop imagining that a mouse pushed me in the shaft."

"This was an accident," Jeff repeated. His eyes looked less dull, her obstinacy stirring a sullen anger. "You know it was yourself."

"Yes," Helen said. "Oh, yes! I was sitting right there. There couldn't be any doubt I'd see for myself that it was an accident."

"What are you driving at?"

"I just wish I could stop remembering things," she said bitterly. "Remembering that I told you and told Nick that if there should be another accident I'd know it was murder. I wish I could stop remembering that. Stop remembering that you both knew that if there were to be another accident it better be good, it better be perfect."

Jeff said, with slow deliberate patience, "You're too tired to know what you're saying."

"Yes," Helen admitted. "It seems I never know when to keep my mouth shut. I was thinking of that yesterday. That's why I kept my mouth shut yesterday."

"Yesterday?" Jeff repeated. He rose.

Price stepped inside to pick up his gray hat from a chair beside the door. He was followed by Nick, who did not look pleasant.

Nick said, "You were retained at a contingent fee for contingent services."

Price said, "I don't need to be told that. And I don't think that you need to be told I'd wash my hands of the lot of you if I could. But as far as Sasoon's concerned I've become tied up with you, these accidents, the whole mess. Only don't count on me letting it go on indefinitely."

Nick was holding his temper. "It won't," he said. "We've come to the end of our stay here. If you can bring the transit out in the morning we can wash things up by night."

"Anything that will hasten your departure," Price said, "I'll be only too pleased to do."

Helen spoke from the foot of the stairs. "Before we start counting on the transit," she said, "perhaps we'd better find out if we have any use for it. We'd better find if we have enough charts to use."

Jeff shrugged irritably.

"Helen's full of mysterious hints," he explained.

Ignoring him, Helen said, "I wish you'd wait until we find out, Mr. Price."

Jeff spoke with forced patience. "I have mine," he listed them. "Nick has his. Sylvia has her father's. That," he counted on his fingers, "makes the three we need."

Helen said, "We'll see if it makes three." she started up the stairs. "I'll get Sylvia and we'll see."

Sylvia had stayed in her room since Willet Price and the deputy sheriff had arrived in mid-morning. She was lying wide-eyed on the bed in a wool dress the same shade of red as her rouged lips. Her red lips were the only color in her face.

"They've gone?" she asked.

"Mr. Price is still here," Helen said.

Sylvia's red lips formed toneless words. "If we only knew the reason," she said. "Any reason for him leaving in the middle of the night . . ." She rolled her head on the pillow, her eyes staring at the ceiling. "If we'd only found the gold in the car . . . or his chart . . . then I could go to sleep," she whispered. "Then I would know it was all right and could stop thinking about the brakes."

Helen picked up a package of cigarettes from the bureau and mangled one out. She kept her back towards the bed.

"Thinking about what?" she asked. Her voice sounded casual enough. Shaky, but casual.

Sylvia said, "I just keep remembering. . . . How one day when I was driving . . . a long straight road . . . no other cars I had to watch . . . just the long straight road . . . and then suddenly I blinked and there was a steep hill in front of me. . . . I jammed on the brakes only barely in time to stop at the top. I'd fallen asleep at the wheel, awoke only just in time. . . ."

There were no matches left. Helen put the cigarette back down on the bureau and faced the bed.

"I haven't been able to get it out of my mind," Sylvia was saying, her voice utterly weary. "For hours and hours. . . . How it would feel to awake in a car that was going down a mountain—to try to put on the brakes and to find that there was something wrong with them, that there weren't any brakes—that there was nothing you could do but try to steer while the car went faster and faster—" her voice ended in a sharp whisper.

She rolled her head on the pillows as if trying to turn away from the thought.

"He was just drunk," she said hopefully. "And he must have hidden them—that's the only reason we couldn't find his chart or the true map we were so sure he'd made. That's the only thing that makes it like the other accidents. But it isn't really like them, it isn't, is it, Helen?" Sylvia raised herself up on her elbow and then sat on the edge of the bed. "What is it?" she asked. "What is it, Helen?"

Helen tried to remember what she had come to see Sylvia about, tried to fix her thoughts upon that.

"The map," she said. "If he had another map it was only a copy of the one we used yesterday. There was nothing wrong with the map we used yesterday." She went to the door. "I'll show you what was wrong."

Downstairs, in the office, Helen took the white window shade from where it was standing in the corner. The others had followed her into the office. Cole had come in from the terrace. He watched from the office doorway.

Helen said, "The charts were cut from this. The first time I saw it, looked at it, the edge had been cut."

Nick Baron took the shade from her. It unwound itself to the floor as he stood holding the raveled edge. He let go of it and kicked the shade out of the way.

"When did you notice this?" he asked.

"Yesterday. Before we surveyed on Mr. Sears's map."

Jeff stooped and picked up the edge of the shade. "If it was cut to start with," he said, "somebody's ripped off a strip since."

"Yes," Nick said, "somebody's ripped off a strip since. Somebody's ripped off a strip of the window shade and then in the privacy of his bedroom has carefully cut out a piece the size of his chart. Then using Saul's typewriter here he's typed out a fake chart. A wooden duck, dear cousin. A decoy."

Jeff was facing Helen.

"You knew before we started?" he asked. "And you let us go on with it?" His voice hardened. "Though you knew that one of the charts was a fake."

"No," Helen said, "I didn't know." She looked at Nick. "I didn't know who had made it. And I so often talk too much."

Nick said thoughtfully, "I'd have got drunk, too. Yes, I think I'd have got drunk, too, if I'd been in Red's shoes. A good map and three charts, and get nowhere." He laughed. "And to think I fell for that 'all cards on the table' act! That open and above-board combining of charts!" He was facing Cole and he was enjoying the joke. "You were typing some—letters—weren't you, Jay? Just before you suggested that we put all our charts on the table?"

Cole was looking at Sylvia. He was looking at no one but Sylvia. He spoke to her and his voice sounded like the air coming out of a rubber balloon.

"It wasn't to deceive you, any one," he said. "A precaution, a mere precaution . . ." The balloon was empty.

Sylvia began ripping an oblong of typed linen. She tore it into narrow strips, not looking at it as she tore it, her face bleak, dead. She stared steadily at her father while, rip after rip, she tore the chart into shreds. She did not speak to him. It was Jeff to whom she turned when she dropped the shreds on the floor.

Her voice was dead. "You didn't want to," she said. "You wouldn't have, except for me. I'm sorry. It simply never occurred to me that my own father would use me as a lure."

She walked past him to the desk with the typewriter. She struck several types together and then, separating the type bars, bent them into a factory repair job. A bright drop of blood ran from a carbon-stained finger when her hands hung at the sides of her red dress.

Nick nodded approval. "We can do nicely without any more wooden ducks," he said, and turned back to Cole. "What've you done with the chart we need?"

"It's in a safe place," Cole breathed. "A very safe place."

"Where?"

"Here. The lodge." Feebly, for a moment, with a faint smile of confident slyness, he looked himself again. "I'm not carrying it on me," he said. "And it isn't in my room. No one can find it."

"That's fine," Nick said. "We don't want any one to find it. We're going to need it in the morning."

Willet Price said, "Miss Farr." Helen turned to him. His dry, gritty voice was refreshing in the way a whiff of a sandstorm would be in the miasmic air of a swamp. "If you'd like for me to drive you in town," he offered, "I'll wait until you pack."

"Thank you," Helen said. "Thank you for giving me the chance . . ."

Thanks for the chance to clear out of this swamp while I'm only a little smirched around the edges, nothing, I guess, that time and clean living shouldn't wash away. Thanks for this one last chance to clear out and leave behind me everything and every one . . .

"Thank you," Helen said again. "But I'm going to stay."

It left an acrid taste in her mouth, but she was too nearly numb to be much troubled about anything in the half hour between Price's departure and the time when she went to sleep, when every one at the lodge went to sleep, just for the novelty. The following nine and a half hours, from two-thirty in the afternoon until midnight, were oblivion.

She was awakened from that oblivion by a confusion of sounds. She smelled smoke when she sat up in bed. She stumbled out of bed for a look into the hall. It was like opening a door in a chimney above a roaring fire. She slammed it shut, staggered towards the back window, choking from the searing blast of smoke. When she got to the window Nick Baron was calling her name outside.

He shouted instructions: "Get some clothes. Come out this way. Don't open your door."

He ran towards the far end of the lodge.

Helen turned back into the room. She bumped into the bureau. She scooped up an armful from the drawers and threw it out the window. She stripped hangers from the bar in the closet, rolling the clothes into a bundle as she returned to the window. She leaned out the window for fresh air.

It was surprisingly peaceful, with a higher moon than the night before. The far corner of the lodge was in silhouette against a red glow. The glow brightened in the second or two that she watched it. Sin came scrambling up the embankment at the corner below her window.

"I'm all right!" she called, shouting at him ten feet away. "See about the others! Hurry!"

Sin hesitated for an instant, sizing up her situation, and then jumped back down the embankment. Helen turned back into the room. There was the sound now as of a wind growing in force. She found her dressing gown on the foot of the bed, mules at the side of the bed. Feeling blindly for shoes in her clothes closet her hand struck her suitcase. She opened it, dropped in three shoes she had been holding in the crook of her arm, found two more. Five shoes. No sense in that. Don't try to save senseless things. Blindly in the darkness she threw out one of the shoes she had dropped in the suitcase, swung her suitcase on top of the bed. Her handbag was on the bureau. She tossed it into the suitcase. She swept the cosmetics on top of the bureau together in her hands.

Suddenly, like the flash of an explosion, there was light in her room. It came from the end window. The fire had swept the length of the hall and was billowing from the open door at the outside stairs. Helen dropped the cosmetics, snapped the suitcase shut and threw it out the window.

She crouched on the window sill, flung herself forward in a frog-like dive. She landed on her hands and knees, sprawled full length. Some one's hands helped raise her shoulders. She sat on her haunches and looked up at John. He had a wide grin.

"Boy!" he said. "Boy oh boy! You ought to go out for track meet."

He gave her shoulder a congratulatory pat and trotted along the embankment to opposite a window midway in the length of the lodge, Nick Baron's window. He leaned across the gap, grasped the window sill and pulled himself into the window.

Helen looked behind her. She had cleared the edge of the embankment by a good five feet. She saw stockings, panties, handkerchiefs, a bra; gathered them into the suitcase. She threw dresses and coats over her shoulders, picked up the suitcase, and then for the first time took a look at the fire, gave some thought to the fire itself.

In the back of her mind she knew that some one had dropped a lamp. The blast of smoke from the hall had reeked with kerosene. The fire had started at the far end of the hall. The cold night air flowing down the mountain had turned the hall into a chimney, or blast furnace. It was roaring now, a blowtorch of fire from the second-floor doorway at her end of the lodge, billows of smoke exploding in flame.

She turned and ran, as fast as she could in mules on rocks, towards the other end of the lodge. The bedroom windows were dark, the fire had not burst through the bedroom doors. As she came abreast of Nick's window John jumped out, picked up some articles of clothing he had thrown ahead of him. She stumbled on past the corner of the lodge, scrambled down a break in the embankment near the shed where the car had been parked, and joined Sylvia, Jeff and Nick standing below the end window of the front bedroom.

Sin came running out of the kitchen door, his arms loaded with a grocery box that he deposited with a pile near the shed. Helen was aware of him only because he nearly ran into her. Bent half double, he skated back under the burning stairs into the kitchen again. John appeared from some place and followed him into the kitchen. Throughout the scene Helen was aware of them shuttling back and forth between the pile of salvage and the kitchen door. Perhaps that was the strangest part of the strange scene, that a lamp was domestically burning on the kitchen table. With the house burning down, it sat there as placidly as Jay Warren Cole stood behind his bedroom window.

That was another strange thing about the scene, that it remained fixed and unchanging like a painting instead of like a moving picture. At this end of the lodge the smoke and flame were blown the other way. The doorway of the upstairs hall was a bright yellow oblong. The landing of the outside stairs and the stairs were burning in orange flame and black smoke. The smoke did not rise in front of Cole's window but swept back up the stairs into the hall doorway. Burning against the draft, the fire was slowly crawling out from either side of the doorway and from the top of the doorway was being whipped back over the ridge of the roof.

Sin skated out of the lamplit kitchen doorway directly below. John, with the grin of a freshman at a football rally bonfire, ran back in again. Nick, hoarse-voiced, continued to shout up at the window, shouting for Cole to jump. Jeff, his face smudged, his blond hair singed, one eyebrow burned off, continued to shout for Cole to jump. Sylvia, in a high flat cry as if hysteria had reached a monotone, continued to call to her father to jump. Cole continued to stand in front of the open window very slowly shaking his head.

Helen thought at first that that was what he was doing, very slowly shaking his head. It was not until something like a half minute of the seemingly interminable scene that she realized that what in fact he was doing was slowly looking back and forth from the hall door of his room at his right to the front window of the bedroom at his left.

The front windows of the set-back second floor of the lodge opened on the roof of the first floor. Helen had had that first-floor roof in the back of her mind. It had been in the back of her mind that Jeff and Cole, the only two remaining at the lodge who had front bedrooms, had only to step out of their windows to the roof, hang by the edge of the roof and drop four or five feet to the ground. But the first-floor roof was afire, was a balcony of flame and smoke across the front of the lodge. It was from that flame-curtained window that Cole slowly turned his head to look down from the window in the end of the lodge in front of which he was standing and then continuing the same slow turn from side to side to look at the closed hall door. Except for that slow, fascinated turning of his head he stood there quite motionless because, Helen Farr suddenly realized, he was paralyzed by fear.

The picture did not change and the sound did not change. There was the roar of the fire and the voices trying to shout above the roar. Then Helen heard John's voice close by her side. She did not look at him but she knew that he was no longer grinning in excitement, that his nice young face would look sick.

He was whispering, defensively, "I thought he'd jump soon's he got warmed up. I thought he'd jump soon's he got warmed up . . ."

The end came without warning. Cole's face, in its changeless swing from side to side, was turned towards the bedroom door. The next thing, he was half out of the window. He hung from the sill by his hands, let go, struck the outer edge of the burning stairs, rolled on the ground. Above him the bedroom exploded into flame.

Nick was the first to reach him. It was too hot to be gentle. He grabbed a wrist and began dragging. Sylvia had started to run forward. Jeff had grasped her, whirled her around and flung her against John, and then had jumped forward to help Nick. Together, they pulled Cole to his feet and carried him between them to the pile of salvage in front of the shed. He hung like a green silk bag between them, making no effort to walk. He was eased down to the ground. Sylvia was on her knees beside him, asking over and over, "Are you hurt? Are you all right? . . ."

Nick said, "He doesn't know."

Helen saw that that was true, he did not know. His eyes were open but he was dazed. She did not feel too bright herself, as she stood there draped in her wardrobe, clutching her suitcase, trying to take in what was happening.

The lamp was still burning in the kitchen, but murkily in the smoke of the burning wreckage of the stairway landing that had fallen to block the doorway. There was Sin, running like a packrat from the pile of salvage to a place over the edge of the terrace that was shielded from the growing heat of the fire. There was John, helping him. There was Jeff, his head bent against the heat, rescuing some clothes that he had dropped where they had been standing before Cole had climbed from the window. There was Cole lying flat on his back, the firelight iridescent on his green silk pajamas, his round face dazed, his round eyes staring straight up at the sky. There was Sylvia kneeling beside him. There was a *whoosh* and an added blaze of heat and light from the lodge. The door of Sylvia's bedroom had given way to the fire.

Helen heard Nick say, "It's broken."

She saw that he had knelt and was looking at Cole's left ankle. The flesh was unbroken but the ankle and the bare foot seemed to puff larger while she looked. She saw Nick staring at Sylvia.

"Good God," he snarled, "it's lucky it's not his neck!"

Helen saw that that was what Sylvia needed. Sylvia had not said anything but her mouth had been open. Sylvia closed her mouth. The look began to go out of her face that had been on it ever since she had been standing beneath her father's window helplessly calling to him to jump. Her body had been stiff as a statue; it began to look like a body again instead of a statue with a nightgown on.

Jeff had come back with his clothes. They were the clothes that he had had on the night before. Only it had been the afternoon before. Exactly half of his face was swollen and inflamed—it was the side with the eyebrow singed off. The eyelash was off too and the eye half closed. It was not Jeff's face from that side. It looked so different that it might have been the face of some one whom she had never seen before.

"We're going to have to move from here," he said. "Damned quickly."

Sylvia was bending over her father.

"There must be something else," she said, her throat still in a tight knot. "His back . . ."

Nick's voice was savage. "The hell with his back. He didn't hit on his back. He hit on his feet on the stairs and fell over on his belly and arms. Maybe an arm, nothing else." He pushed Sylvia out of the way and ran his hands over Cole's arms. "They feel all right. Hell, he's all right except for his ankle!" He took Sylvia by her shoulders, stood her on her feet. "He's all right," he shouted into her face. "It's just shock. It'll wear off." He turned to Jeff. "Can we tie it up some way before we carry him?"

Helen saw Jeff shake his head, heard him say. "Might do more harm than good." She watched him sit down and begin putting on his shoes. She looked down at her own feet. She had had on mules. She was surprised to see that she did not have any on now. Her toenails were not painted but they appeared painted in the red blaze of the fire. She looked at Sylvia's feet. Her toenails were painted. Sylvia had on one mule. Sylvia was always losing just one mule.

"Sylvia," she said, "you've lost a mule."

It sounded exactly as it would have had she said, "Sylvia, your slip's showing." It sounded crazy, but she knew she was not crazy because she was on her knees opening the suitcase, throwing around lingerie, hunting for the two pairs of shoes she had put in the suitcase. If it had sounded like a crazy thing to say it was only because she had not been thinking about what she said. It was only because she had been wanting to scream: *How did the fire start?*

"Around my room."

Helen did think she was crazy. You are crazy if you do ask questions and only learn that you have asked them when some one replies to them. Besides, she was staring at the four shoes she had found. Her walking shoes and one black and one blue shoe. It had been crazy to throw that fifth shoe away in the dark. She looked up from the shoes. Jeff had stopped midway in pulling his trousers over his pajamas. Nick was standing beside Sylvia with his arms full of clothes. His own clothes and a lot of Sylvia's clothes. John had saved them. Including shoes. Sylvia was holding shoes. Sylvia was holding the shoes as though she had just taken them from Nick and then both of them had been frozen that way, as Jeff was frozen.

"A wall of flame around my room."

Jay Warren Cole's voice was a dear, calm monotone.

"I knew you were going to burn me to death," he said. "I knew you were going to burn me to death when I heard you on the roof outside my window. I knew you were pouring kerosene on the roof. I could smell the kerosene. I was awake. I had been waiting for you."

His round face was calm. It was more than calm, it was placid.

"I knew you would come to kill me," he said. "I'd known you were going to kill me ever since you killed Red when I left him alone in the car last night. When I went into the lodge to get my chart so that Red and I could find Saul's gold. I knew you'd killed him to keep us from finding the gold."

He was looking straight ahead, straight up, with clear, untroubled eyes.

"I don't know how you killed Red," he said. "I didn't know how you were going to kill me. I thought you'd come into the room. I thought you'd come into the room and come to the bed and kill me while I was asleep. That's why I pinned the chart on top of the blankets," he explained.

Helen was staring at his eyes. He was not speaking to all of those who stood around him. He was speaking to one of them. She was waiting for him to look at the person to whom he was speaking.

"But of course you didn't know," he said. "You didn't know I'd realized my mistake. The mistake I'd made when I'd told you that my chart was hidden where no one could find it. I'd been drinking too much after Red was killed. I'd been drinking too much or I'd have realized sooner that you already had more than enough charts to find the gold. Your own," he said methodically, "and Harry's and Helen's and Red's. More than enough."

Helen had stopped hearing the roar of the fire that was so loud it made it hard to hear his quiet voice.

"I should have realized sooner," he said, "that you wanted another chart only in order to keep the rest of us from finding the gold. To keep us from finding it before you had time to locate it and dig it up and carry it away. A thousand pounds of minted gold. A great deal of work. It would take time. But you would have all the time in the world if there were only two charts left for the rest of us. You didn't have to have my chart. It would be enough if no one could find it. And no one could find it if I was dead. I realized what a mistake I had made in telling you that. That is why I got the chart from where I had hidden it and pinned it to the outside of the blankets when I went to bed. When you came to kill me I hoped you might just take the chart instead."

Staring at him lying in front of her, Helen saw him lying in bed, his face round and white in the moonlight, the dark blankets pulled up to his chin, the white oblong of the chart pinned to the blankets. Just lying there, waiting to be murdered, too broken by fear to resist.

"I heard you," he said again. "First in the hall, and then you bumped into something in Red's room, and then I heard you outside my window on the roof. Then you went back again. But I could smell the kerosene. I knew you were going to burn me to death. And then it came. The wall of flame around my room. I expected to die, but I am safe. I am not in danger any more. Because I haven't got a chart any more. It's pinned to a blanket in my room."

Then, at last, his eyes moved. He turned his head and looked at the blazing window of his room. He smiled as peacefully as a placid child.

Sin grasped Helen by the shoulder, shouted into her face:

"You gone clazy?" he shrieked. He flung her suitcase down the side of the terrace, grabbed an armful of clothes. The heat from the fire was hot enough to broil. Helen jerked her arm loose from Sin as he tried to pull her away.

Sylvia had dropped to her knees beside Cole, her face bent over his.

"Who was it, father?" she asked. "Who was it!"

Cole slowly looked from Jeff Oliphant to Nick Baron. He said, with a happy smile, "I don't know."

11

Carrying her suitcase, her wardrobe draped over her shoulders, Helen walked with bent head, and fast. At the point where she reached the road there were no more than wisps of smoke from the black cloud that billowed overhead, a black cloud in a red light. The lodge was a torch for the procession following her in a wide circle around it to the road. Its strong but unsteady light gave a jerky, hopping motion to the figures of the procession, as if Nick and Jeff were bouncing Cole up and down as they carried him between them, and the lantern that Sylvia carried to give secure light to their footsteps seemed to blaze up and down with the light of the fire. Some distance behind them a grocery box floated redly above a pool of shadow where Sin with bent knees and back shuffled beneath it unseen except for a pale glint of moonlight on the barrel of his carbine. Farther back, John was staggering under the double burden of carrying a wash boiler full of salvage and keeping in play the unnecessary, stabbing, cold white beam of a flashlight.

Helen did not look back again until she reached the stampmill. Far up the road the lantern had come to a stop: Cole was a heavy burden. Somewhat nearer the white shaft of the flashlight jabbed down the road, spotted Sin sitting on the grocery box, came to a stop beside him. Helen went to the far end of the mill where it made a windbreak against the cool night wind, a shadow in the red glare of the fire, a shadow filled with the soft silver of the moon. Now that she had hurried ahead there was nothing to do but to wait: wait for them, wait for the morning, wait for the end.

It was not much past seven-thirty, and a diamond of a morning, when Willet Price drove up with the surveyor's transit in his touring car. He had promised that he would leave Sasoon about six o'clock, and since no one walking from the mine could have reached there by that time, no one had been sent, but it was a relief if not a surprise to find him as good as his word. Jay Warren Cole's foot and ankle were bad.

But as Helen looked at him as he sat at one end of the back seat, his green silk-clad arms bracing him to either side, his legs stretched out on the seat, his foot swathed in wet cloths that had once been her pajamas, his round face flushed with fever and drawn with pain, as he sat there beaming upon them and a little drunk, he was, she thought, magnificent.

He was magnificent because he was something that she never expected to be: he was himself again. In the long, silent, waiting hours of that night that had drained the last of hope and heart out of her he had put himself together again. Lying there at the back of the mill throbbing with pain only a little dulled by a salvaged bottle of whisky, he had picked himself up from the broken thing that had nearly let itself be burned to death and had put Jay Warren Cole together again as good as new. Even better. It had been about four in the morning, when the only blaze of fire to be seen in the night was that of their campfire boiling a pot of coffee, that he had announced the improvement.

"Retire," he had said, and patted Sylvia's hand. "I shall retire . . . A chicken ranch! To live in the wholesome innocence of the pastoral life . . . Ah, my dear young friends, there is no satisfaction as sweet as the sweat of honest toil . . ."

He could afford to be patronizing. The pride that had pulled him together again might have seemed a little queer in other circumstances. It was his pride in the knowledge that Sylvia knew that he was not a murderer.

It beamed from him as he kindly patted John on top of his pork-pie hat and said, "Good boy." John was the one other person who was smiling. He was sitting on the floor of the car in charge of a canteen of water for the swathings of Cole's foot and what was left of the bottle of whisky for the dulling of his pain. Red and green plaid ankles pushing white and brown sports shoes against his suit-case, the socks matching the handkerchief in the pocket of his sports coat, a thimble-bowled pipe, collegiate and unburnable, sticking at a jaunty angle from his mouth, he gave no evidence of sorrow at parting from his grand-uncle Sin or indication of regret that this summer vacation job, like a blind date with a maniac, was over.

Jay Warren Cole beamed at Jeff, who had offered to drive them in and drive the car back for the second and final load, but Jeff sat woodenly behind the wheel, staring straight ahead. He beamed at Willet Price, but the law-yer, standing at the side of the road a little back from the rest of them, looked as aloof and affable as a cactus. He beamed at Sin, but Sin was shuffling back to the camp at the stampmill and did not turn his head. He beamed at Nick Baron, but not for long, seeing in his face that morning a little too much of Saul. It was better not to think about the past. He beamed at Sylvia sitting beside Jeff, the tripod of the transit aslant between her and the door, but Sylvia was leaning around the tripod to face Helen.

"There's room," she said. "We can put this some place else."

Helen shook her head. "I'll wait," she said. "I want to say good-by to Billy." It wouldn't even help you for me to go, she thought. It wouldn't make it any easier for you to sit beside Jeff, not knowing if he is the one who is innocent or if he is the murderer.

They looked into each other's bleak eyes.

"In town, then," Sylvia said.

"Yes, dear." Helen stepped back from the car. She saw Jay Warren Cole beaming at her. She smiled back. "Good-by!"

The car was out of sight. Helen turned and there were Nick and Willet Price. She did not look at Nick. Price had doffed his hat in farewell to Sylvia, still held it in his hand. As he stood facing Helen she saw again the tall sun-dried man in a gray business suit, gray hat in hand, his hair pewter-gray in the sharp white sunlight, who had stood in front of her when she first had stepped from the train in Sasoon. She remembered his hostile courtesy and she remembered the scene in his office, only now she thought that she understood it a little better.

Helen said, her voice small on the mountainside, "At least you tried to let me know what I was in for, tried to warn me."

Price said dryly, "I thought you might find your company here a little outside of your experience." He bowed slightly, excusing himself. "I think I'll take a look at the ashes." He put on his hat and started up the road.

Helen had no intention of being left alone with Nick. She stepped quickly past him. As she walked down the side of the mill she heard his voice and Price's on the road to the lodge. Sin was squatting near what was left of the campfire. He was pouring beer from a can into a steaming cup of coffee. Intent on sniffing it, he did not look up as she went on by and started down the trail to Billy Bedrock's.

Billy was at his forge putting a fresh point on a prospecting pick, a hammer with a long pick point. When the wavy blue temper lines suited his experienced eye he doused the pick and came forward to meet her, the steam still rising from the cooling steel. He stopped smiling after getting a good look at her face.

Helen said, "The lodge burned down last night. Mr. Cole was hurt," she went on, getting through with it. "Broke his ankle. He's been taken to town in Mr. Price's car. When it comes back," this was the hard part of it, "when it comes back I'll be leaving too. All of us." His face was blurred.

"You'd better come in and sit down, Miss," Billy said gently. "You look played out."

"I guess I am," Helen said. She sat down at the table. "I guess just about everything is."

Billy put his hat and the prospecting pick on the table, stood looking down at them.

"You won't be coming back?" he asked, knowing the answer.

"No," Helen said. "No."

Billy said, "I'd kind of got used to having you here. When you get old you kind of get used to people quick, I guess."

"You don't have to be old, Billy." She was sitting very straight, holding herself up that way with her arms on the table, the palms of her hands pressed flat and hard against the table.

"You had anything to eat?" Billy asked.

Helen shook her head. "Sin cooked breakfast. But I wasn't hungry."

"Hard to eat sometimes," Billy said; "crowd of people around."

"The—people—who were around may have had something to do with it," Helen admitted.

Billy went to the stove. "What you need's a stack of hot pan cakes," he said. "And some wild-bee honey. Got a sting to it." He pushed a simmering pot of beans to the back of the stove, put some wood in the firebox, rolled up his sleeves. "It's broke a lot of hearts, Dead Finger," she heard him say. "Sometimes I'm near sorry I ever found it."

"Don't think that," Helen told him. "It's not the mine. We lied to you about the mine. We haven't been looking at the mine. We've just been looking for . . . some gold."

Billy dipped some flour from a keg into a bowl.

"I know," he said. "It can break your heart. The way it keeps leading you on."

Sitting very straight in the chair, her head a little back, Helen looked in Saul Baron's eyes, smiling at her from his photograph on the shelf.

"Yes," she said. "Yes, you can be led on until it breaks your heart."

Billy said, "And now you're leaving. . . . And we never did get to go nugget hunting together."

"I know, Billy. And I'm sorry. I'll always be sorry."

Billy had a happy thought. "The car won't be back very soon, will it?" he asked. Helen shook her head. It would be five hours or more. They'd have to crawl over the rough road going in. "Then if you got nothing you got to do maybe we can look for a color or two this morning?"

"No," Helen admitted, staring at the top of the table, "I've nothing I've got to do." Nothing but wait. Wait for Jeff to come back. Wait for the end. The hat and the prospecting pick swam together. "But I'm afraid I wouldn't be much good at it this morning, Billy," she said. "Must have to have pretty good eyes to spot those little nuggets! Mine, mine don't seem much good somehow this morning. No good at all."

Billy came to the side of the table.

"Maybe," he said, "they're good enough to spot little colors like this."

Something round and golden swam in front of her eyes. On the table, in a dust of flour, was lying a twenty-dollar gold piece. Billy gently patted her shoulder.

"There's gold here, all right," he said. "More'n an old man has any use for. You just have to know where to find it."

Nick and Willet Price were waiting for Sin to boil a fresh pot of coffee when Helen returned to the mill. Billy was with her. He gave a long look up the ridge at the blackened chimneys that were the only things remaining of the lodge.

Sin grinned evilly. "You gotta haul own glub now. Bet by God you miss me."

"Well, I don't know," Billy said doubtfully. "I never missed you before I knew you."

"How are you going to make out up here alone?" Nick asked.

Helen was glad to hear him speak to Billy. She had avoided looking at him but out of the corner of her eye she had seen him looking at her. She was afraid she couldn't be looking quite the same as before she had gone to Billy's, even if it was a good idea to try to. She heard Billy explain that he had Mr. Parsons' burro.

"It's a trip," he confessed. "But you get to do a bit of prospecting on the way." He absently dug up a piece of rock with the prospecting pick, broke it, squinted at a streak of iron.

"Too bad you haven't a car."

Billy let the piece of rock roll out of his hand. "Why . . ." he said, discovering the simplicity of the idea, "I've only got to learn how to drive!"

Willet Price said, as if to kill the idea while it was young and before Billy had known it long enough to become too attached to it, "A car costs money."

Billy nodded. "Gold's worth money."

Price said patiently, "The cheapest outfit you could nurse over this road would cost you as much as you find in six months."

Nick said, "That's what you think." Helen looked at him then, she looked at him quick. He was smiling at Billy. "A hundred dollars from one shower," he said. "Yes, I wouldn't be surprised if you could afford a car."

Billy nodded. "A nice new shiny one," he said, squinting at it, "with red wheels."

Helen said quickly, "Billy's going to take me gold hunting now. There's time, before Jeff . . ." She stopped speaking as Nick faced her.

"Never give up, do you?" he asked. His lip curled out in a smile, his eyes remaining hard and bright. "Best of luck!" he said. "Be nice if you could find some gold you can take away with you. A nugget's a nice keepsake."

Helen said, "I'm sure I shall." She hated his smile. Her lips felt tight as she returned his smile. "In fact," she said, stretching the smile, "Billy's promised to show me a place where I'll find nuggets as big as twenty-dollar gold pieces." She gave the smile another stretch and then turned to Billy. "Didn't you?"

Billy was not smiling any more. He said quietly, and gravely, "I'll show you where to look for them."

Willet Price watched them cross the bed of the gulch and disappear over the other side.

"I don't like the way he talked," he said. "As if he believed it. I didn't know Billy'd been talking like this."

Nick smiled, dismissing it. "Seems a harmless delusion."

Price continued to frown. "These old prospectors all go a little queer," he said. "Too many years of living alone with a fixed idea. Mr. Parsons got crazy as a coot. He was far from harmless."

At the shafthead on First Strike, Helen turned for a long look back. Only the top of the stampmill could be seen, the wreckage where the skip had carried Harry McIntyre to death. There was no one in sight. No one had followed them.

She said, "I guess we can go in, Billy."

She followed him past the rusted ore car that sat midway between the shafthead and the point where the tracks
dipped down into the inclined shaft. It was, Billy explained, called an inclined shaft because it was a tunnel
that dipped down, one foot in ten it dipped, though he'd
tried to tell them . . .

Helen pulled up with a start. A match had flared in
front of her eyes. Billy was lighting a candle. Billy was
saying something about a "drift." She wondered what he
had been saying while she had been walking in a trance.
She looked around her, for the first time seeing what she
looked at. Rusty rails slanting into darkness ahead, square
wood posts supporting a plank roof, wet, rock walls—that
was the cold chill she felt.

Billy was still talking. He was holding the candle at the
entrance to a tunnel that branched off at right angles. It was
a much narrower tunnel and very short, not over twelve feet
long. The wet rock at the end of the tunnel was a smooth
pasty green. The rock of the tunnel was a rough brown.

Billy's gentle voice was saying, "Like I was saying, these
drifts was to show how the width of the ore body was holding out, and then at the end there's a pot hole about four
feet deep." The floor of the drift was covered with water.
It looked black. Billy kicked a pipe that ran along one wall
and under the water. "For the pumps," he explained. "Kept
the drain into the pot holes pumped out. Kept the water
from mounting up."

Helen spoke very carefully to keep from shrieking.
"Please, Billy," she said. "Please hurry."

Billy smiled. "You see how it is," he said. "You see
how it is that nobody else could be interested in fooling
around this old tunnel but me."

Helen followed him, the candle, into the darkness
ahead. There was a seep of water along one wall. She

slipped on the wet rock, grasped at his shoulder, nearly fell as he stooped to pick up a stick about four feet long lying against the rusted rail. Another hundred feet and they stood at the edge of water, from wall to wall, stretching away out of sight.

"Reached its level two years ago," Billy said. His soft voice whispered back in echo over the water. "Saul knew a thing or two." He gave Helen the candle and the prospecting pick. "You better hold these." He picked up a tin can near the water's edge. It was just a battered tin can not worth a second glance. A battered tin can with two rough holes jabbed through its sides. A prospecting pick could have made the holes. Billy began screwing the stick through the holes. "It's back at the last drift we passed," he said.

It was not far back to the drift, twenty or thirty feet. There was the light of the candle, and then there was a long stretch of blackness, and then there was a small, bright doorway to the day. Then she was facing the entrance to the drift. It was just like the first one that Billy had shown her. Only this time Billy waded into the water. It was over his shoetops when he stopped four or five feet from the end. He stood looking down at the water in front of him.

When Helen heard his voice she felt that he was far away from her. Much farther in time and space than the eight or nine feet he seemed to be.

"Wasn't sense, wading in here," he said. "No sensible reason on earth for doing it. Wasn't sense, getting down on my knees and holding the candle around until I could see down into the pothole. Wasn't sense, I had to get so almighty curious about that pile of loose rock in the bottom I had to stick my arm in clear over the shoulder to poke at it with my pick. No sensible man on earth would have done those things . . . or seen his pick come up with a little rotten canvas sticking to it and then under the rock that'd been knocked aside seen the gold."

He laughed softly. Helen wished he wouldn't. It made her back prickle.

"Wasn't sense for sure," Billy said. "Only an old fool would have done it. An old fool who'd always known there was gold here at Dead Finger if he just kept looking everywhere long enough for it. Besides, I'd heard stories about Saul."

To Helen's astonishment he turned his head and winked at her. It was hard to take in for a moment. That he had not been mooning about the guiding hand of some visionary faith but was, and for years had been, enjoying a huge and very practical joke.

Billy bent over and pushed the tin can on the end of the stick down into the water.

"Not that I've needed much," he said. "It's almost nearly all here. I'd been saving it for Saul." He was scooping with the can. "Makes me happier, though, that I've been saving it for you."

Helen did not hear him. She had heard a footstep quite close in the shaft. She turned and said, her voice dead, "So it's you, Nick."

"Why, no, Miss Farr."

Willet Price loomed into the candlelight, came to a stop where he could look past her into the drift. Helen stared at him blankly, conscious of only an unbelievable, stunned relief. Billy had straightened, was facing them. He let loose of the stick. It was pulled down under the water. Price looked at Helen again.

"No," he said, "Mr. Baron's still at the mill. He seemed to think that I was unduly alarmed when I told him I was uneasy about you being alone with Billy. Despite Billy's clearly unbalanced state of mind."

Helen said, "You don't understand! It's the gold, Mr. Price. Billy's found the gold."

Willet Price said dryly, "A clear case of insanity. Homicidal insanity. It explains everything that's happened here.

It's fortunate that I was uneasy, as I told Mr. Baron, and felt I should keep an eye on you. It's fortunate that when you weren't in sight I correctly surmised where to find you."

Helen understood, then. She took a step back, was backed against the corner of the shaft and the drift.

Willet Price spoke his next thought: "It's unfortunate that I didn't get here in time to save you from his maniacal attack."

Billy came forward one step and came to a stop when he saw the revolver pointed at his stomach. Helen felt bony fingers close over hers, effortlessly twist the prospecting pick out of them. Hot tallow dripped from the candle on the fingers of her other hand.

His next thought: "I had to shoot him in self-defense."

Helen did not feel the hot tallow from the candle. She was no longer conscious that she was holding the candle. She was conscious only of the gaunt face in the candle-light, as merciless as the dry voice that was saying what it would say to the world outside:

"But he had already killed you."

Helen watched the long point of the prospecting pick swing up and back. It was like the head of a snake. There was a sharp but muffled sound. It had no meaning to her until the pick struck, not at her, but aside, spearing the candle from her hand, bringing blackness: that sharp but muffled sound had been a shot from the head of the inclined shaft.

The revolver exploded in front of her eyes. Hands grasped her shoulders, pulling her down. Somehow she knew that it was Billy. She was kneeling. His hands pressed insistently against her shoulders. She was lying flat on her stomach in the water in the drift. Her head and shoulders were outside the drift. She could hear Billy breathing close beside her. There was nothing else to hear.

She could see nothing in the blackness around her. She could see through the blackness up to the oblong of sunlight at the far end of the inclined shaft. She had just time to take it in that that was all that she saw when there was a jet flame from the opposite side of the shaft some twenty feet ahead of her and the sound of the shot slapped against her ears. She saw a dark shape pass between her and the oblong of light. She saw a pinpoint flash from near the head of the shaft. She heard the thud of the bullet into one of the timbers on the opposite side of the shaft and heard the sharp, muffled report of the shot. In silhouette against the light she saw a dark figure moving up the shaft. From the far end of the shaft there came back to her, distorted by echoes, a muffled, shrill yelling of unintelligible words. It was Sin's voice.

They were cut short by the slam of the revolver and Price again leaped to the opposite side of the shaft as he fired. There was again the pinpoint flash near the head of the shaft, the slap of a bullet where Price had been standing. There was the sing of a ricochet and a splash of water from down the shaft.

Helen's gaze was fixed on the place where she had seen the pinpoint flash of the rifle. Sin was there. She saw that he should not be there. There was too much light. Willet Price would be able to see him before he could see Willet Price. She wanted to yell to him to run, but she saw that he couldn't run. If he tried to move from the wall he would be in silhouette against the light. He was trapped.

Price crossed the shaft again. In silhouette against the light she could see him slipping along the wall, slipping up for the kill.

Helen got to her knees, her feet, struggled to break loose from Billy. A queer, low, groaning sound ran through the blackness in front of her. Against the bright oblong of sunlight at the head of the shaft there loomed the shape of the ore car. It moved down the tracks, gathering speed. The white beam of a flashlight plunged ahead of it like a headlight.

Price had fired twice before he turned and ran. He fired again directly in front of the drift, ran on. It was not until his feet splashed into the standing water that he realized that he had run past the drift. Helen saw him turn. The light was coming as fast as that. He aimed, fired. The bullet bonged against the ore car as it rocketed past the mouth of the drift. For an instant Helen saw him standing at the edge of the water full in the white beam of the flash-light. She saw the black mark that suddenly appeared in the middle of his forehead. Then the ore car hit the water. There was a roof-high curtain of water. The beam of the flashlight pointed straight up as the ore car sea-sledded for forty feet before turning over. A man was standing to his waist in water.

"Helen!" Nick yelled.

The flashlight found her, came bobbing nearer as Nick plowed through the water. When he came up to her he grabbed her arm.

"Damn you," he said.

He swung her around by his grip of her arm and took her along with him towards daylight. Helen did not try to pull away from his hand. It hurt her arm but it gave a good deal of support and her knees could use a good deal. Sin came skating into the beam of the flashlight, swinging his carbine in front of him like a hockey stick. His face was a grinning walnut shell. It grinned at Nick.

"Tank attack O. K.!" he complimented.

Nick said, "Nice shot, Sin. Very nice. Perhaps you and Billy'd better pull him out of the water." He gave the flash-light to Billy, said to him, "I don't want to guess where . . . something . . . is. You're going to show me. Voluntarily. Later."

Helen stood in the sunlight. Nick was still holding her arm. She wished he would let go so she could sit down. Instead he shook her.

"God only knows why you're still alive!" he said. He shook her again.

Helen said, "Stop shaking me like a wet dog!" She jerked her arm away from him, pulled her sopping dress away from her where it was sticking the closest. "My hero!" she blazed. "You might have come a little sooner instead of nearly letting us all be murdered in our sleep!"

Nick held his temper. "Sin threatened to shoot me if I didn't stay back when he started to follow Price," he said. "I had to keep my distance, out of sight."

Helen remembered what had nearly happened and felt rotten again. That was the way it had been ever since she had been at Dead Finger. Feel rotten or mad enough to bite. Take your pick. Now she felt rotten, remembering.

"I couldn't believe it," she said. "That it was he. He hadn't even been here most of the time."

"No," Nick said. "He just drove out at night. Parked his car down the road. Strolled over and did the necessary. And drove back home again, well before dawn."

Helen said. "He was here the first night." Her voice was quick and tense, thinking it out, remembering. "He was the one who guessed there must be something hidden in the photographs. He tore up mine, but it was the wrong one. He tried to get Jeff's, but Jeff had thrown his out the window. Then, later—it was he who took the map from the office!—who," she gave a shaky laugh, "and again he was disappointed!"

Nick again put his hand on her arm.

"But he didn't give up, did he?" Helen asked. "No. He had more luck when he caught Harry McIntyre. More luck when he pushed me in the shaft. And then he stole the surveying things, to keep us from finding the gold, to give him time to kill—" she broke off.

"Yes," Nick said. "You want to thank God the lodge burned down. That Jay told us how Red was killed. Because it's the only reason you're still alive!" His temper was like a lump of dough that he was holding too tight. Some of it was beginning to squeeze out. "I'm not psychic," he said. "I'd believed the only thing that seemed possible about Red. That he'd taken a drunken whim to drive to town. I'd kept on believing that if Jay hadn't told us that the only reason Red was even in the car was that he was just sitting there waiting for Jay to get his chart so they could find the gold together! Red wouldn't pick that moment to take a ride somewhere. The only other answer was that he had been taken for a ride. Some one had driven him down there, hopped out, and turned the car off the road. But all the rest of us had been at the lodge, all the rest of us who were mixed up in this, all of us except Price."

Nick's hand had tightened on her arm again. The skin was drawn tight over the beak of his hawk nose. Helen did not know. She saw Willet Price turning the car off the road, running to his own parked car, driving back to town. She saw him waiting for the message that Billy had brought in the morning. She saw him in the office when Jay had told them that his chart was not in his room but was hidden somewhere in the lodge where no one could find it. She saw him drive back to town and wait for night and then again drive out his car and come stealing up to the lodge. She saw him go to the shed and take the five-gallon can of kerosene for the lamps. She saw him strike the match for the wall of flame that was to keep Cole from running from his room to save his chart. Helen saw the dry smile with which Willet Price must have loaded the surveyor's level in his car that morning, knowing that they could not use it with only Nick's and Jeff's charts left to them, knowing

that when he reached the mine he would find them burned
out and ready to leave, to leave him alone to take at his
leisure Saul Baron's gold. . . .

"You knew," she said. "You knew and you didn't tell
me!" Helen felt his hand on her arm now. It hurt.

"Tell you?" Nick asked. "Have you forgotten you hav-
en't been speaking to me for a couple of days. Against your
scruples, I suppose! How the hell could I tell you? Besides,
it was just possible that it was Billy. I wanted to find out
if he could drive a car. That's all I wanted to do, find if he
could drive a car, but you"—he shook her—"with that one-
track, gold-crazy mind of yours, you have to start talking
about nuggets as big as twenty-dollar gold pieces! With
what you have on your mind, no wonder your hair's got
gold in it! My God! But remember this, it's only a miracle
that we're not all as dead as dodos, with Price thinking up
an airtight explanation and keeping the gold for himself."

Helen stood facing him rigidly. Nick took his hand
from her arm.

"Yes," she said. "Yes, that would be what would be wor-
rying you. The gold. Well, you can have it. All of it. I
don't want it. I wouldn't touch it with a ten-foot pole. I've
stayed here because I had to, had to learn something. I'd
always felt that when the gold was found I'd learn who'd
done these things." Her voice went very low. "And who . . .
hadn't. I had to know."

Nick said, "Why, you poor little fool."

"Fool! Fool? Oh, I suppose you can't help it. I suppose
that after enough years with some financial swindle house
you can't help but look upon everybody else as a fool." She
beat at him with words: "Do you think I was saying anything, one word, at the mill that I hadn't planned to say?
Don't you know I tried to make it as clear as I could that
Billy had found the gold and was going to show me where
it was? Don't you think I knew that whoever had the charts

knew where the gold was, at least about where it was, and that he'd follow us to see if we went there? Don't you realize I had to find out if you would follow?"

Nick said, "Why, you poor little fool. Why didn't you tell me you loved me?"

"Sylvia," Helen said. "It was for Sylvia and Jeff, I had to find out, for Sylvia, if it— Oh, have Billy show you where the gold is! And let me go!"

Nick held on to her arm. He held on to both arms.

"Why, you poor little fool," he said. "Don't you know, yet, that Uncle Saul had a sense of humor?"

"Lovely people," Helen said, thin-lipped. "You and your Uncle Saul. Lovely."

Nick's lower lip was curled out in a grin. "We have a sense of humor," he said. "The letter I received from Uncle Saul inviting me here was addressed to my place of business. That Philly financial house I'm with happens to be the U.S. Treasury Department."

Helen got it, slowly. "Then . . . he knew . . ." she said.

Nick's head nodded, close above hers. "Yes," he said. "Saul knew. How much of what has happened here did he know was going to happen, I don't know. I think he just left it up to our worser natures, including the lawyer who'd failed to keep him out of prison. But at least he did know that the gold had been forfeit when he had failed to declare it under the provisions of the gold law."

Helen got a little more of it. "And you," she said, "you knew too—that even if we found the gold, we weren't going to get it!"

"Why, you poor little fool," Nick said, "why else do you think I've been trying to persuade you to pull out of here ever since you got here? I've been trying to keep you from being disappointed, maybe killed, for nothing. And as I've told you before," he said, "you're too beautiful to die."

Sin and Billy came out of the shaft. Billy, with innate courtesy, turned and looked back down the shaft. He did not think the nice young lady would tell any one about his flour keg. Maybe he'd better not 'Malgam Method too fast, even though he'd been sending gold to the same assay office for forty years, but even if he had to learn to drive a second-hand car it could still have red wheels.

Sin tapped them on the arm. "Bleak it up," he said. "Like lookee these?"

Nick said, "Of all the times . . ." He looked at soggy pieces of linen that were the charts, a section of the map that had hung in the office. "No, hell no," he said. "Not now."

Helen disengaged a hand and put in on Sin's arm.

"You've got to go with us," she said.

Sin's nose wrinkled in distaste. "Plenty soon you have squall-face wet dliapa," he prophesied. "All time laise hell, maik woik."

COACHWHIP PUBLICATIONS
ALSO AVAILABLE

SULTAN'S HAREM MYSTERY

Drink the Green Water
The Milkmaid's Millions

HUGH AUSTIN

COACHWHIP PUBLICATIONS
ALSO AVAILABLE

SCHOLAR TURNS DETECTIVE
IN TWO SOPHISTICATED MYSTERIES

MURDER IN THE ZOO
MURDER IN CHURCH

Babette Hughes

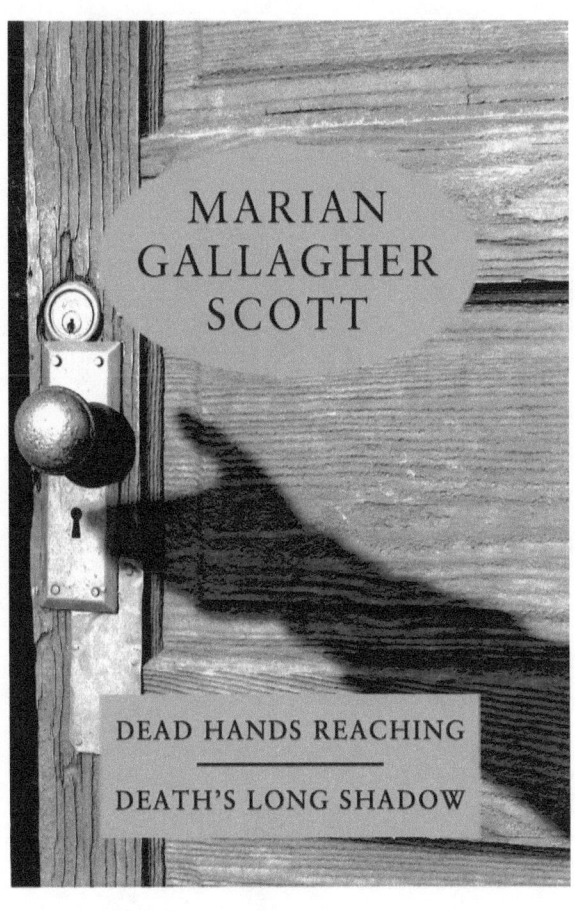

MARIAN
GALLAGHER
SCOTT

DEAD HANDS REACHING

DEATH'S LONG SHADOW

COACHWHIP PUBLICATIONS
ALSO AVAILABLE

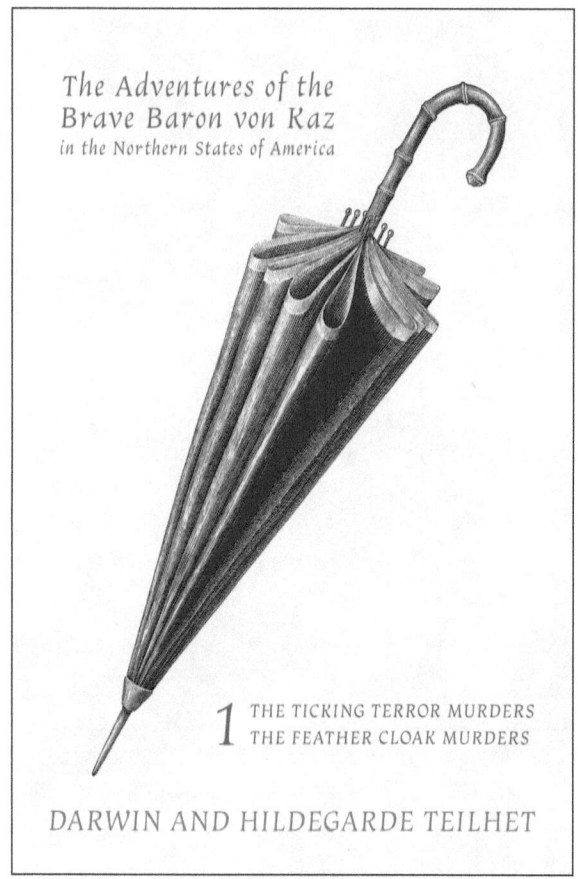

The Adventures of the
Brave Baron von Kaz
in the Northern States of America

1 THE TICKING TERROR MURDERS
THE FEATHER CLOAK MURDERS

DARWIN AND HILDEGARDE TEILHET

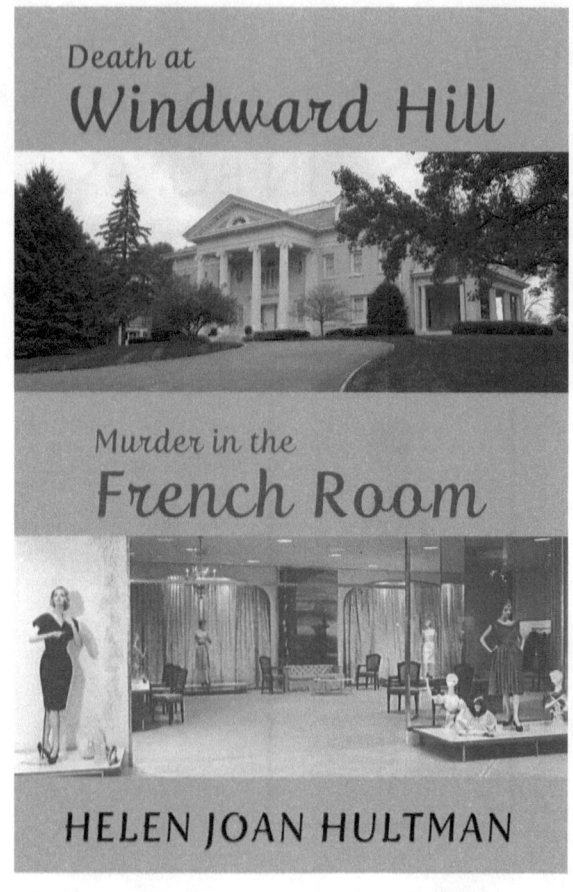

NARROW
GAUGE TO
MURDER

CAROLYN THOMAS

COACHWHIP PUBLICATIONS
ALSO AVAILABLE

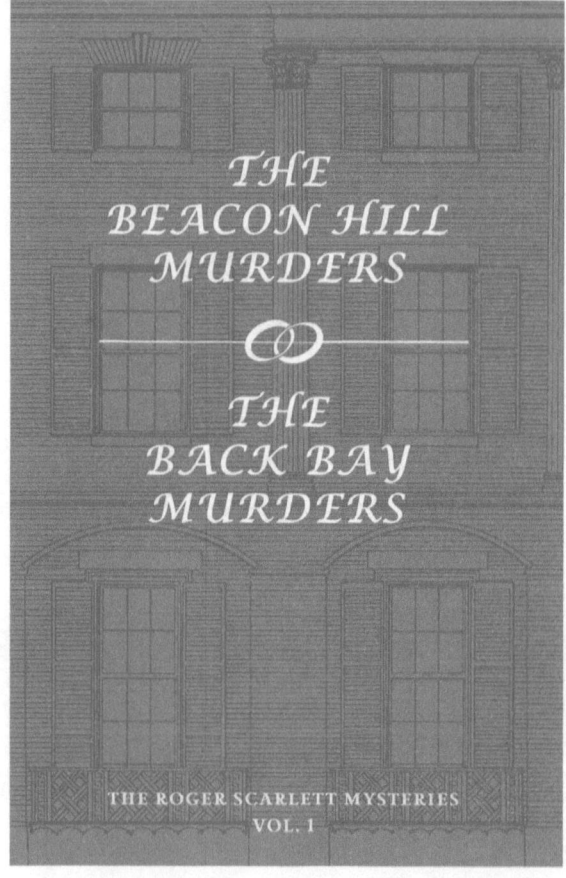

THE
BEACON HILL
MURDERS

∞

THE
BACK BAY
MURDERS

THE ROGER SCARLETT MYSTERIES
VOL. 1

COACHWHIPBOOKS.COM (PRINT)
COACHWHIP.COM (EPUB)

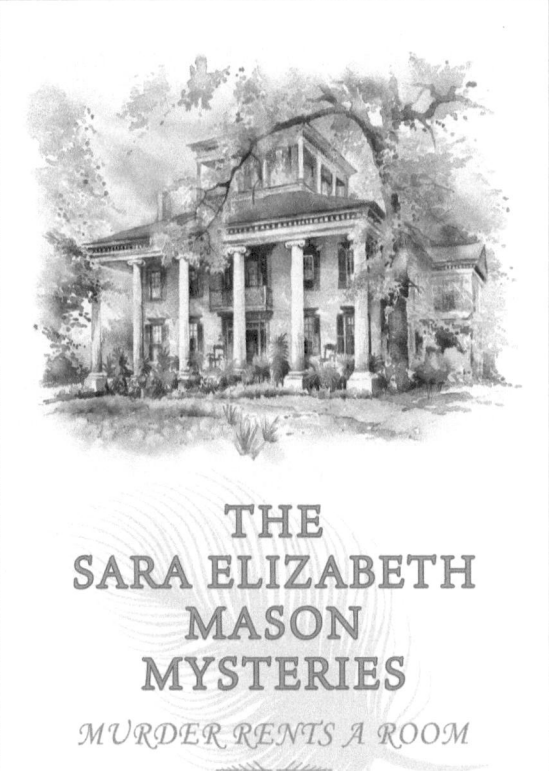

THE
SARA ELIZABETH
MASON
MYSTERIES

MURDER RENTS A ROOM

»»»—«««

THE CRIMSON FEATHER